D0727855

FIVE GET INTO A FIX

Five Get
Into A Fix

Enid Blyton

**Hodder
Children's
Books**

a division of Hodder Headline plc

First published in Great Britain in 1958
by Hodder and Stoughton

This edition 1991

The right of Enid Blyton to be identified as the Author of
the Work has been asserted by her in accordance with the
Copyright, Designs and Patents Act 1988.

For further information on Enid Blyton
please contact w.w.w.blyton.com

20 19 18 17 16

A catalogue record for this title is available from the
British Library

ISBN 0-340-54891-6

Printed and bound in Great Britain

Hodder Children's Books
a Division of Hodder Headline plc
338 Euston Road
London NW1 3BH

Contents

1 A miserable Christmas 7
2 Off to Magga Glen 14
3 The end of the journey 21
4 In the old farmhouse 28
5 Things might be worse! 35
6 A funny little creature 42
7 Back at the farm again 49
8 Off to the little hut 56
9 A strange tale 63
10 In the middle of the night 69
11 Strange happenings 76
12 Out on the hills 83
13 Aily is surprising 90
14 Morgan is surprising too 97
15 'What's up, Tim?' 104
16 Aily changes her mind 111
17 The 'big, big hole' 118
18 Inside Old Towers 125
19 A lot of excitement 132
20 In the heart of the hill 140
21 An astounding thing 147
22 All's well that ends well! 154

1 A miserable Christmas

'I do think these Christmas holidays have been the worst we've ever had,' said Dick.

'Bad luck on George, coming to stay with us for Christmas – and then us all going down with those awful colds and coughs,' said Julian.

'Yes – and being in bed on Christmas Day was *horrible*,' said George. 'The worst of it was I couldn't *eat* anything. Fancy not being hungry on Christmas Day! I never thought that would happen to *me*!'

'Timmy was the only one of us who didn't get ill,' said Anne, patting him. 'You were a pet, Tim, when we were in bed. You divided your time between us nicely.'

'Woof!' said Timmy, rather solemnly. He hadn't been at all happy this Christmas. To have four of the five in bed, coughing and sneezing, was quite unheard of!

'Well, anyhow, we're all up again,' said Dick. 'Though my legs don't really feel as if they belong to me yet!'

'Oh – do *yours* feel like that too?' asked George. 'I was quite worried about mine!'

'We all feel the same,' said Julian, 'but we shall be quite different in a day or two – now we're up. Anyway – we get back to school next week – so we'd *better* feel all right!'

Everyone groaned – and then coughed. 'That's the

worst of this germ we've had, whatever it is,' said George. 'If we laugh – or speak loudly – or groan – we start coughing. I shall go completely mad if I don't get rid of my cough. It keeps me awake for hours at night!'

Anne went to the window. 'It's been snowing again,' she said. 'Not much – but it looks lovely. To think we might have been out in it all last week. I do think it's too bad to have holidays like this.'

George joined her at the window. A car drew up outside and a burly, merry-looking man got out and hurried up the steps to the front door.

'Here's the doctor,' said Anne. 'I bet he'll say we're all quite all right to go back to school next week!'

In a minute or two the door opened and the doctor came into the room, with the mother of Julian, Dick and Anne. She looked tired – and no wonder! Looking after four ill children and a most miserable dog over Christmas had not been an easy job!

'Well, here they are – all up and about now!' said Mrs Barnard. 'They look pretty down in the mouth, don't they?'

'Oh – they'll soon perk up,' said Dr Drew, sitting down and looking at each of the four in turn. 'George looks the worst – not so strong as the others, I suppose.'

George went red with annoyance, and Dick chuckled. 'Poor George is the weakling of the family,' he said. 'She had the highest temperature, the worst cough, and the loudest groans, and she . . .'

But whatever else he was going to say was lost beneath the biggest cushion in the room, which an angry George had flung at him with all her might. Dick flung it back, and everyone began to laugh, George too. That set all the four coughing, of course, and the doctor put his hands to his ears.

'*Will* they be well enough to go to school, Doctor?' asked Mrs Barnard anxiously.

'Well, yes – they would – but they ought to get rid of those coughs first,' said the doctor. He looked out of the window at the snow. 'I wonder now – no – I don't suppose it's possible – but . . .'

'But what?' said Dick, pricking up his ears at once. 'Going to send us to Switzerland for a skiing holiday, Doc? Fine! Absolutely smashing!'

The doctor laughed. 'You're going too fast!' he said. 'No – I wasn't actually thinking of Switzerland – but perhaps somewhere hilly, not far from the sea. Somewhere really bracing, but not *too* cold – where the snow will lie, so that you can toboggan and ski, but without travelling as far as Switzerland. Switzerland is expensive, you know!'

'Yes. I suppose it is,' said Julian. 'No – we can't expect a holiday in Switzerland just because we've had beastly colds! But I must say a week somewhere would be jolly nice!'

'Oh *yes*!' said George, her eyes shining. 'It would *really* make up for these miserable holidays! Do you mean all by ourselves, Doctor? We'd love that.'

'Well, no – someone ought to be there, surely,' said Dr Drew. 'But that's up to your parents.'

'I think it's a jolly good idea,' said Julian. 'Mother – don't *you* think so? I'm sure you're longing to be rid of us for a while. You look worn out!'

His mother smiled. 'Well – if it's what you need – a short holiday somewhere to get rid of your coughs – you must have it. And I won't say that I shan't enjoy a little rest while you're enjoying yourselves having a good time! I'll talk it over with your father.'

'Woof!' said Timmy, looking inquiringly at the doctor, both ears pricked high.

'He says – *he* needs a rest somewhere too,' explained George. 'He wants to know if he can come with us.'

'Let's have a look at your tongue, Timmy, and give me your paw to feel if it's too hot or not,' said Dr Drew, gravely. He held out his hand, and Timmy obediently put his paw into it.

The four children laughed – and immediately began to cough again. How they coughed! The doctor shook his head at them. 'What a din! I shouldn't have made you laugh. Now I shan't be coming to see you again until just before you go back to school. I expect your mother will let me know when that day comes. Good-bye till then – and have a good time, wherever you go!'

'We will!' said Julian. 'And thanks for bothering about us so much. We'll send you a card when our coughs are gone!'

As soon as Dr Drew had driven off in his car, there was a conference. 'We *can* go off somewhere, can't we, Mother?' said Dick, eagerly. 'The sooner the better! You must be tired to death of our coughs, night and day!'

'Yes. I think you *must* go somewhere for a week or ten days,' said his mother. 'But the question is – *where*? You could go off to George's home, I suppose – Kirrin Cottage . . . but it's not high up . . . and besides, George's father would certainly not welcome four coughs like yours!'

'No. He'd go mad at once,' said George. 'He'd fling open his study door – and stride into our room – and shout "Who's mak—"'

But as George began to shout, she coughed – and that was the end of her little piece of acting! 'That's enough, George,' said her aunt. 'For goodness sake, go and get a drink of water.'

There was much debating about where they could

go for a little while, and all the time they were talking the snow fell steadily. Dick went to the window, pleased. 'If *only* we could find a place high up on a hill, just as the doctor said, a place where we could use our toboggans, and our skis,' he said. 'Gosh, it makes me feel better already to think of it. I do hope this snow goes on and on.'

'I think I'd better ring up a travel agency and see if they can offer us something sensible,' said his mother. 'Maybe a summer camp set up on a hill would do – it would be empty now, and you could have a choice of a hut or a chalet or something.'

But all her telephoning came to nothing! 'No,' said the agencies. 'Sorry – we haven't anything to suggest. Our camps are all closed down now. No – we know of no winter ones in this country at all!'

And then, as so often happens, the problem was suddenly solved by somebody no one had thought of asking . . . Jenkins, the old man who helped in the garden! There was nothing for him to do that day except sweep a path through the snow. He saw the children watching him from the window, grinned and came up to them.

'How are you?' he shouted. 'Would you like some apples? They've ripened nicely now, those late ones. Your mother said you weren't feeling like apples – or pears either. But maybe you're ready for some now.'

'Yes! We are!' shouted Julian, not daring to open the window in case his mother came in and was angry to see him standing with his head out in the cold. 'Bring them in, Jenkins. Come and talk to us!'

So old Jenkins came in, carrying a basket of ripe, yellow apples, and some plump, brown-yellow pears.

'And how are you now?' he said, in his soft Welsh voice, for he came from the Welsh mountains. 'You're pale, and thin too. Ah, it's the mountain air of Wales you want!'

He smiled all over his wrinkled brown face, handing round his basket. The children helped themselves to the fruit.

'Mountain air – that's what the doctor ordered!' said Julian, biting into a juicy pear. 'I suppose you don't know somewhere like that we could go to, do you, Jenkins?'

'Well, my aunt lets rooms in the summertime!' said Jenkins. 'And she's a good cook, my Aunt Glenys. But I don't know if she'd do it in the wintertime, what with the snow and all. Her farm's on the hillside, and the slope runs right down to the sea. A fine place it is in the summer – but there'll be nothing but snow there now.'

'But – it sounds *exactly* right,' said Anne, delighted. 'Doesn't it, Ju? Let's call Mother! Mother! Mother, where are you?'

Her mother came running in, afraid that one of the children was feeling ill again. She was most astonished to see old Jenkins there – and even more astonished to hear the four children pouring out what he had just told them. Timmy added a few excited barks, and Jenkins stood twirling his old hat, quite overcome.

The excitement made Julian and Dick cough distressingly. 'Now listen to me,' said their mother, firmly. 'Go straight upstairs and take another dose of your cough medicine. *I'll* talk to Jenkins and find out what all this is about. No – don't interrupt, Dick. GO!'

They went at once, and left their mother talking to the bewildered man. 'Blow this cough!' said Dick, pouring out his usual dose. 'Gosh. I hope Mother fixes up something with Jenkins's aunt. If I don't go off somewhere and lose this cough, I shall go mad – stark, staring mad!'

'I bet we'll go to his old aunt,' said Julian. 'That's if she'll take us. It's the kind of sudden idea that clicks – don't you think so?'

Julian was right. The idea did 'click'. His mother had actually met Jenkins's old aunt that spring, when she had come to visit her relations, and Jenkins had brought her proudly up to the house to introduce her. So when Dick and Julian went downstairs again, they were met with good news.

'I'm telephoning Jenkins's aunt, old Mrs Jones,' said their mother. 'And if she'll take you – well, off you can go in a day or two – coughs and all!'

2 Off to Magga Glen

Everything was soon settled. Old Mrs Jones, whose voice came remarkably clearly over the long-distance line, seemed delighted to take the four children.

'Yes, I understand. Oh, their coughs won't last a day here, don't you worry. And how's my nephew, Ivor Jenkins?'

'Mother! Tell her we're bringing a dog, too,' said Julian, in his mother's ear. George had been making wild gestures to him, pointing first to Timmy, then to the telephone, where her aunt stood patiently listening to old Mrs Jones's gossipy talk.

'Oh – er – Mrs Jones – there'll be a dog, too!' said her aunt. 'What – you've seven dogs already? Good gracious! Oh, for the sheep, of course . . .'

'*Seven* dogs, Timmy!' said George, in a low voice to Tim, who wagged his tail at once. 'What do you think of that? Seven! You'll have the time of your life!'

'Sh!' said Julian, seeing his mother glance crossly at George. He felt thankful that this unexpected holiday had been so quickly fixed up. Like the others, he was beginning to feel very down and dull. It would be wonderful to go away. He wondered where their skis were . . .

Everyone looked brighter when things had been settled. No school for some time! No lounging about the house wishing something would happen! Timmy would be able to go for long walks at last. They would be on their own again, too, a thing the Five loved.

Jenkins was very helpful in looking out toboggans and skis. He brought them all into the house to be examined and cleaned. Something exciting to do at last! Their exertions made them all cough badly, but they didn't mind so much now.

'Only two days to wait – then we're off!' said Dick. 'Ought we to take our skates, do you think?'

'No. Jenkins says there's no skating round about the farm,' said George. 'I asked him. I say – look at that mound of woollen clothes your mother's just brought in, Ju! We might be going to the North Pole!'

'Whew, Mother! If we wear all those, we'll never be able to ski!' said Julian. 'Gosh, look – *six* scarves! Even if *Timmy* wears one, that's one too many.'

'One or two may get wet,' said his mother. 'It won't matter how many clothes you take – you're going by car, and we can easily get everything in.'

'I'll take my field-glasses, too,' said Dick. 'You never know when they might be useful. George, old think, I do hope Timmy will be friends with the farm dogs. It would be awful if he quarrelled with them – and he does sometimes get fierce with other dogs, you know – especially if we make a fuss of them!'

'He'll behave *perfectly*,' said George. 'And there's no *need* to make a fuss of other dogs if we've got Timmy.'

'All right, teacher!' said Dick, and George stopped her polishing and threw her duster at him. Yes – certainly things were getting normal again!

When the time came for the children to set out on their journey they were feeling a good deal better – though their coughs were still almost as bad! 'I do hope you'll lose those awful coughs, Julian, before you come back,' said his mother. 'It worries me to hear you all cough, cough, cough, day and night!'

'Poor old Mother – you *have* had a time!' said Julian, giving her a hug. 'You've been great. What a sigh of relief you'll give when we're all safely away in the car!'

At last the car came, driving up the snowy path to the house. It was a hired car, a very big one, and that was fortunate, as the children's luggage was truly colossal! The driver was a cheerful man, and he and Jenkins soon had the suitcases, toboggans, skis and all the rest either in the boot of the car, or strapped on top.

'There we are!' said the driver at last. 'Everything made fast. We're making a nice early start, and we should be safe in Magga Glen before it's dark.'

'We're all ready to start!' said Julian and the man nodded and smiled, climbing into the driving seat. Dick sat beside him, and the other three sat at the back, with Timmy on their feet. Not that he would stay there long! He liked to look out of the window just as much as the children did!

Everyone heaved a sigh of relief as the car slid down the drive. They were off at last! Jenkins was at the gate, and waved as they went past.

'Remember me to my old aunt now!' he shouted, as he shut the gate.

The driver was very chatty. He soon heard all about their miserable holidays, and how much they were looking forward to their unexpected break before going back to school. In return he told them all about himself and his family – and as he had eleven brothers and sisters, his tale lasted for a good part of the journey!

They stopped for a meal in the car after some time, and found that they were hungry for the first time since they had been ill.

'Good gracious – I can really *taste* these sandwiches!' said George, in a surprised voice. 'Can you, Anne?'

'Yes – they don't taste of cardboard – like all our meals have lately,' said Anne. 'Timmy – you're not going to fare so well, now that we're getting our appetites back!'

'He was a very good dustbin while we were ill, wasn't he?' said Dick. 'He simply *gobbled* up all the bits and pieces we couldn't eat. Ugh – that boiled fish! It tasted like stewed knitting!'

They laughed – and that set them off coughing again. The driver listened and shook his head. 'Nasty coughs you've got!' he said. 'Reminds me of the time when me and my family got whooping-cough – twelve of us together. My, when we all whooped, it sounded like a lot of fire-sirens going off!'

That made the children laugh again, and cough. But somehow nobody minded the irritating coughs now – they would surely soon be gone, once they could get out into the country and try their legs at running and racing and skiing once again.

It was a long drive. All the children fell asleep in the car after their meal, and the driver smiled to see them lolling back against one another, looking very peaceful. Only Timmy was awake, and he climbed cautiously up between George and the window, wishing the window was open, so that he could put his big nose out into the wind, as he loved to do.

They stopped for a very early tea at a tea shop in a village. 'Better stretch your legs a bit,' said the driver, getting out. 'I know I want to stretch mine. Look – I'm going into that place over there for my tea. There's plenty of my pals there, and I'd enjoy a chat. You go and tuck in at this tea shop here, and ask for their buttered crumpets. They're the best in the world! Be back for you in a quarter of an hour – not longer, or we shan't be at the farmhouse before dark. It's still about an hour's run, but there'll be a moon later on.'

They were all glad to stretch their legs. Timmy bounded out as if he were on springs, barking madly. He was disappointed to find that they were only making a short stop – he had hoped they were at the end of their journey. But he was pleased to be given a buttery crumpet all to himself in the tea shop. He licked every scrap of butter off first, much to the children's amusement.

'I'd rather like to do that myself, Timmy,' said Anne. 'But it's not really good manners, you know! Oh, *don't* make my shoe buttery – take your crumpet a bit farther away.'

They had time for two crumpets each, and a cup of hot tea. Julian bought some chocolate biscuits, as he felt unexpectedly hungry, even after two crumpets.

'Marvellous to feel even a *bit* hungry, after not being able to look even bread and butter in the face!' he said. 'I knew we must be jolly ill that day we couldn't eat even ice-cream though Mother tried to tempt us with some!'

'My legs are still a bit funny,' said Anne, walking back to the car. 'But they're beginning to feel as if they *belong* to me, thank goodness!'

They set off again. They were in Wales now, and mountains were beginning to loom up in the distance. It was a very clear evening, and although the mountains were white with snow, the countryside they passed was not nearly as snowy as their own home had been when they left.

'I hope to goodness the snow doesn't begin to melt, just as we've arrived,' said Dick. 'It seems all right up on the mountains at present – but down here in the valleys there's hardly any.'

They passed a signpost, and Julian looked to see

what it said. He made out a word that looked like Cymryhlli, and called to the driver.

'Did you see that signpost? Should we look out for Magga Glen now?'

'Yes. We must be getting on that way,' said the driver. 'I've been looking out for it myself. I wonder I haven't seen it yet.'

'Goodness! I hope we haven't lost our way,' said Anne. 'It will soon be dark.'

The car went on and on. 'Better look out for a village,' said Julian. But they didn't come to one – nor did they see any other signposts. The night was now coming on, but there was already a small moon, which gave a little light.

'Are you sure we're right?' Dick asked the driver. 'The road seems to be getting a bit rough – and we haven't passed even a farmhouse for ages.'

'Well – maybe we are on the wrong road,' admitted the driver, slowing down. 'Though where we took the wrong turning I simply don't know! I reckon we're near the sea now.'

'Look – there's a turning up to the right!' shouted George, as they went slowly on. 'It's got a signpost, too!'

They stopped by the signpost, which was only a small one. 'It doesn't say Magga Glen,' said Dick, disappointed. 'It says Old Towers – just that. Would it be the name of a place, do you think – or a building? Where's a map?'

The driver hadn't one. 'I don't usually need a map,' he said. 'But this countryside isn't signposted as it should be, and I wish I'd brought my map with me. I guess we'd better turn right and go up to see this Old Towers. Maybe they can put us on our road!'

So they swung up to the right, and the car went

slowly, crawling up a long, steep, winding road.

'It's quite a mountain,' said Anne, peering out of the window. 'Oh – I can see something – a building on the side of the hill, look – with towers. This must be it.'

They came to stout wooden gates. On them was a large notice, with just two words on it in large black letters:

KEEP OUT

'Well – that's nice and polite!' said the driver, angrily. 'Keep out! Why should we? Wait a bit – there's a little lodge here. I'll go and ask our way.'

But the lodge was no more helpful than the big gate. It was in complete darkness, and when the driver banged on the door, there was no answer at all. Now what could they do?

3 The end of the journey

'Well – we'd better turn round and go back down the hill,' said Dick, as the driver came back to the car.

'No, wait, I'll just hop out and see if there are any lights anywhere,' said Julian, and jumped out of the car. 'I could go up the drive a little way and see if I can spot the house itself. It can't be *very* far. After all, we spotted it just now as we came up the winding road.'

He went to the gates, and looked at them in the light from the car's headlamps. 'They're padlocked,' he called. 'But I think I can climb over. There's certainly a light somewhere beyond – though how far, I don't know.'

But before he could climb over the gate there came the sound of running footsteps behind it – and then a loud and savage howl came on the night air, and some animal hurled against the other side of the gate.

The driver got back hurriedly into the car and slammed the door. Julian also ran to the car, finding his legs could go quickly if he wanted them to, for all their feebleness!

Timmy began to bark fiercely, and tried to leap through the closed car window. The howling and barking behind the gates went on and on, and the dog there, which must have been a very big one, continually hurled itself against the gates, shaking them from top to bottom.

'Better turn round and go,' said the driver, scared.

'Whew! I'm glad I'm this side of those gates. What a din! That dog of yours is almost as bad, too!'

Timmy was certainly furious. Why wasn't he allowed to get out and tell the other dog what he thought of him? George tried to pacify him, but he wouldn't stop barking. The driver began to turn the car round, cautiously backing a little and then going forward, and backing again. The road was fairly wide, but there was a very steep slope to the right of the car. Old Towers was certainly built on a mountainside!

'The people there must be jolly scared of burglars to have a dog like that,' said Dick. 'Yet it's such a lonely place you wouldn't think many people would come near it. What's up, driver?'

'There's something wrong,' said the driver, who now had the car facing back down the road again. 'The car seems very heavy to drive, all of a sudden. As if I'd got my brakes on.'

'Perhaps you have,' said Julian.

'Well, I haven't,' said the driver, shortly. 'That is, only just a little, to make sure the car doesn't shoot off down the hill – you can see it's pretty steep here, and there's almost a cliff, your side. Don't want to drive down *there* in the dark! What *can* be the matter with the car? It will only crawl.'

'I thought it came *up* the hill terribly slowly, too,' said Dick. 'I know the road was steep and winding – but didn't it seem to *you* as if the car was making heavy work of it?'

'Well, yes, it did,' admitted the driver. 'But I just thought the hill must be steeper than I imagined. What *is* the matter with the car? I've got no brake on at all, and I'm pushing the accelerator down hard – and still she crawls! As if she'd got a ton weight to pull!'

It really was a puzzle. Julian felt worried. He didn't

want them to have to spend the night in the car, lost in a cold countryside – especially as now it was beginning to snow lightly! The moon had disappeared behind heavy clouds, and everything looked very dark indeed.

They reached the bottom of the hill at last, and came on to the level road again. The driver heaved a sigh of relief – and then gave a sudden exclamation.

'What's happened? The car's all right again! She's going like a bird! Whew – that's a load off my mind! I thought she was going to pack up, and leave us to spend the night here.'

The car sped along well now, and everyone was most relieved. 'Must have been something wrong with her works somewhere,' said the driver. 'But I'm blessed if I know what it was! Now – look out for a house or a signpost.'

They actually came to a signpost not long after that, and George yelled out at once. 'Stop! Here's a signpost. STOP!'

The car slid to a stop beside it, and everyone looked at it and gave a shout of delight. 'Magga Glen! Hurrah!'

'Up to the left,' said the driver, and swung his car into the lane. It was rather rough, and obviously only a farm road – but there, right up the hill they were now climbing, was a house, with lights shining in the windows. That must be old Mrs Jones's farmhouse.

'Thank goodness!' said Julian. 'This must be it. I'm glad we got here before the snow set in properly. It's quite difficult to see through the windscreen now.'

Yes – it was the farmhouse. Dogs set up a terrific barking as the car drew near, and Timmy at once answered, almost deafening everyone in the car!

The driver drew up at the farmhouse door, and

looked out cautiously to make sure that none of the
barking dogs was leaping about round the car. The
front door opened, and framed in the light stood a little
old woman, as upright as any of the children!

'Come in, come in!' she called. 'Out of this cold and
snow! Morgan will help with the luggage. Come in,
now!'

The four children, suddenly feeling very tired, got
out of the car. Anne almost stumbled, because once
again her legs felt as if they didn't belong to her, and
Julian caught her arm. They went in wearily, only
Timmy seeming to have any energy! A tall man
hurried out to help the driver with the luggage, salut-
ing them as he passed.

The old lady took them into a big warm living room
and made them sit down. 'What a journey for you!' she
said. 'You look worn out and poorly. It's late too, and
I had a good tea laid for you. But now it's supper you'll
be wanting, poor children!'

Julian caught sight of a loaded table not far from the
fire, set to one side. Although he was tired, the sight of
the good food there made him suddenly feel hungry.
He smiled at the kind old woman. Her hair gleamed
like silver, and her fine old face was wrinkled all over –
but her eyes were as sharp and bright as a blackbird's.

'I'm sorry we're so late,' he said. 'We lost our way.
This is my sister Anne – this is our cousin George – and
this is my brother Dick.'

'And this is Timmy,' said George, and Timmy at
once offered his paw to the old woman.

'Well, now, it's a wonder to see a dog with such
good manners,' she said. 'We've seven – but not one of
them would shake hands – no, not if the Queen herself
came here, God bless her!'

The barking of the dogs had now died down. Not

one of them was to be seen in the house, and the children thought they must be outside in kennels somewhere. Timmy trotted about round the room, sniffing into every corner with much interest. Finally he went to the table, put his paws up and had a good look at the food there. Then he went to George and whined.

'He says he likes the look of the food there,' George said to the old woman. 'I must say I agree with him! It looks good!'

'Go and wash and get yourselves a bit tidy, while I make some hot tea,' said Mrs Jones. 'You look cold and hungry. Go through that door, look – and up the little flight of stairs. The rooms up there are all yours – no one will disturb you.'

The Five went out of the door and found themselves in a little stone passage, lit by a candle. A narrow flight of stone steps led upwards to a small landing on which another candle burned. The steps were very steep, and the children stumbled up them, their legs stiff after their long drive.

Two bedrooms opened off the little landing, opposite to one another. They seemed exactly alike, and were furnished in the same way too. There were washstands with basins, and in each basin was a jug of hot water, wrapped around with a towel. Wood fires burned in the little stone fireplaces, their flames lighting the rooms almost more than the single candles there.

'You'll have this room, girls, and Dick and I will have the other,' said Julian. 'Gosh – wood fires in our bedrooms! What a treat!'

'I shall go to bed early, and lie and watch the flames,' said Anne. 'I'm glad the rooms aren't cold. I know I should cough if they were.'

'We haven't coughed *quite* so much today,' said Dick, and immediately, of course, had a very bad fit of coughing! The old woman downstairs heard him, and called up at once.

'You hurry up, now, and come down into the warm!'

They were soon downstairs, sitting in the warm living room. Nobody was there except old Mrs Jones, pouring out tea.

'Isn't anyone else coming in to tea?' asked George, looking all round. 'Surely all this food isn't just for us?'

'Oh yes it is,' said the old woman, cutting some ham in long thin slices. 'This is your own room – the room I let out to families for themselves. We've got our big kitchen over there for ourselves. You can do what you like here – make as much noise as you like – no one will hear you – our stone walls are so thick!'

After she had served them, she went out of the room, nodding and smiling. The children looked at one another.

'I like her very much,' said Anne. 'How old she must be, if she is Jenkins's aunt! But her eyes are so bright and young!'

'I feel better already,' said Dick, tucking into the ham. 'George, give Timmy something. He keeps poking me with his paw, and I really can't spare him any of my ham.'

'He can have some of mine,' said George. 'I thought I was hungry – but I'm not, after all. I suddenly feel tired.'

Julian looked at her. She did look tired, and her eyes were ringed with black shadows. 'Finish your meal, old thing,' said Julian, 'and go up to bed. You can unpack tomorrow. You're tired out with the long drive! Anne doesn't look nearly so tired as you do!'

Old Mrs Jones came in again, and approved highly of Julian's idea that they should all go up to bed when they had finished. 'Get up tomorrow when you like,' she said. 'And just come into my kitchen and tell me when you're down. You can do just what you like here!'

But all they wanted to do at that moment was to get into bed and go to sleep by the light of the crackling wood fires! What a relief it was to slip in between the rather rough sheets and shut their eyes! All except Timmy. He kept guard by the door for a long time before he crept on to George's bed. Good old Timmy!

4   In the old farmhouse

The four children slept like logs all night long. If they coughed they didn't know it! They lay in their beds, hardly moving – and only Timmy opened an eye occasionally, as he always did on the first night in a strange place.

He jumped when a burning log fell to one side in the fireplace. He stared sternly at a big bright flame licking up the chimney, as the log burned fiercely. He cocked up an ear when an owl hooted outside the window.

But at last he too fell asleep, lying as usual on George's feet – though old Mrs Jones would not have approved of that at all!

Julian awoke first in the morning. He heard the sounds of the farm coming through the closed window. Shouts of one man to another – the lowing of cows – the barking of one dog after another, and then all together – and the peaceful sound of hens clucking and ducks quacking. It was nice to lie and hear it all, feeling warm and lazy.

He looked at his watch. Good gracious, it was almost nine o'clock! Whatever *would* Mrs Jones think of them. He leapt out of bed, and awoke Dick with the quick movement.

'It's almost nine!' said Julian, and went to the washstand. This time there was only cold water in the big china jug, but he didn't mind. The bedroom was still warm with the burnt-out wood fires. The sun shone outside, but in the night the snow must have fallen heavily, for everywhere was white.

'Good,' said Julian, looking out. 'We shall be able to use our toboggans soon. Wake the girls, Dick.'

But the girls were already awake, for Timmy had heard the boys stirring, and had gone whining to the door. George stretched herself, feeling quite different from the night before.

'Anne – how do you feel? I feel really fine!' said George, pleased. 'Do you know it's nine o'clock? We've slept for more than twelve hours. No wonder we feel better!'

'Yes. I certainly do too,' said Anne, with an enormous yawn. 'Oh look, I've made Timmy yawn too! Timmy, did *you* sleep well?'

'Woof!' said Timmy, and pawed impatiently at the door. 'He wants his breakfast,' said George. 'I wonder what there is. I feel rather like bacon and egg – goodness, I thought I'd *never* feel like eating that again. Brrrr – this water's cold to wash in.'

They all went downstairs together and found their living room warm with a great wood fire. Breakfast was laid, but only a big crusty loaf, butter and home-made marmalade were there, with an enormous jug of cold, creamy milk.

Mrs Jones came in almost at once, beaming at them. 'Well, good morning to you now,' she said, 'and a nice morning it is too, for all the snow we had in the night. What would you like for breakfast now? Ham and eggs – or home-made pork sausages – or meat patties – or . . .'

'I'd like ham and eggs,' said Julian, at once, and the others said the same. Mrs Jones went out of the room, and the children rubbed their hands.

'I feared we were only going to have bread and

butter and marmalade,' said Dick. 'I say, look at the cream on the top of this milk! Me for a farm life when I grow up!'

'Woof!' said Timmy, approvingly. He kept hearing the other dogs barking, and going to the windows to look out. George laughed at him. 'You'll have to remember you're just a visitor, when you meet those dogs,' she said. 'No throwing your weight about, and barking your head off!'

'They look pretty big dogs,' said Dick, joining Timmy at the window. 'Welsh collies, I should think – they're so good with the sheep. I say, I wonder what that dog was that barked at us so fiercely last night, behind that gate at Old Towers? Do you remember?'

'Yes. I didn't much like it,' said Anne. 'It was rather like a nasty dream – losing our way – going up that steep hill – only to find that horrid notice on the gates – and nobody to ask the way – and then that hidden dog barking ferociously just the other side of the gates! And then the car *crawling* down the hill in that strange way.'

'Yes. It *was* a bit strange,' said Dick. 'Ah – here comes our breakfast. Mrs Jones, you've brought in enough for eight people, not four!'

She was followed by an enormous man, with a mass of black hair, bright blue eyes, and a stern mouth.

'This is my son, Morgan,' she said. The four children looked at the giantlike man in awe.

'Good morning,' said Julian and Dick together, and Morgan nodded his head, after giving them one quick look. The girls gave him polite smiles, and he nodded at them too, but didn't speak a word. He went out at once.

'He's not much of a one for talking,' said the old

woman. 'Not my Morgan. But the voice he's got when he's angry! I'm telling the truth when I say you could hear him a mile away! Sends the sheep skittering off for miles when he shouts!'

Julian felt that he could quite believe it. 'Those are his dogs you can hear barking,' said the old woman. 'Three of them. They go about with my Morgan everywhere. He's all for dogs, he is. Doesn't care much about people! He's got four more dogs on the hills with the sheep – and, believe you me, if Morgan went out in the yard there, and shouted, those four dogs with the sheep on the hills far away would hear him and come tearing down here like a flash of lightning!'

The children felt as if they could well believe this of the giantlike Morgan. They rather wished he *would* call his dogs. His voice would certainly be worth hearing!

They set to work on their breakfast, and although they couldn't eat quite all that Mrs Jones had brought, they managed to do very well indeed! So did Timmy. They especially liked the bread, which was home-made and very good.

'I could really make a meal just of this home-made bread and fresh butter,' said Anne. 'Our bread at home doesn't taste a bit the same. I say – wouldn't Mother be amazed to see the breakfast we've eaten today?'

'She certainly would – considering that we haven't felt like eating even a boiled egg for days,' said Dick. 'I say – oughtn't we to telephone home, Julian, and say we're safely here?'

'Gosh, yes,' said Julian. 'I meant to last night. I'll do that now, if Mrs Jones will let me. Hallo, look – isn't that our last night's driver going off. He must have spent the night here.'

The driver was about to get into his car when he heard Julian knocking at the window. He came over to the farmhouse, and walked in at the front door, and soon found the children's living room.

'I'm just off,' he announced. 'The old lady gave me a bed in the barn last night – never been so cosy in my life! And I say – I've found out why the car crawled so slowly up and down that hill to Old Towers last night!'

'Oh, have you? Why was it then?' asked Julian, with interest.

'Well, it wasn't anything to do with the *car*,' said the driver, 'and wasn't I thankful to know that! It was to do with the hill itself.'

'Whatever do you mean?' said Dick, puzzled.

'Well, the shepherd's wife told me they think there must be something magnetic down under that hill,' said the driver. 'Because when the postman goes up on his bicycle, the same thing happens. His bicycle feels like lead, so heavy that he can't even cycle up – and if he *pushes* his bike, it feels just as heavy too. So now he leaves his bike at the bottom and just walks up!'

'I see – so the magnetic whatever-it-is got hold of the car last night, and pulled so much that it made it go slow too,' said Julian. 'Peculiar! There must be some deposit of powerful metal in that hill. Does it affect all cars like that?'

'Oh yes – no one goes up there in a car if they can help it,' said the driver. 'Funny thing, isn't it? Odd hill altogether, if you ask me – that notice on the gate and all!'

'I wonder who lives there?' said Dick.

'Only an old lady,' said the driver. 'She's off her head, so they say – won't let anyone in! Well – *we* know that all right. Sorry I lost my way last night – but you're all right now. You're in clover here!'

He moved to the door, raised his hand in salute, and went out. They saw him through the window getting into his car and driving away, waving a leather-gloved hand out of the window.

'Is the snow thick enough to toboggan on?' wondered George. 'It doesn't look like it. Let's go out and see. Better wrap up well though – I bet the wind's cold out on this hill, and I don't want to start sniffling again. I've had enough of that.'

Soon they were all clad in heavy coats, scarves and woollen hats. Mrs Jones nodded her head when she saw them, and smiled. 'Sensible children you are,' she said. 'It's cold today, with a biting wind, but healthy weather! Be careful of that dog of yours, my boy – don't you let him loose till you're well away from the farm, in case he goes for one of my Morgan's dogs.'

George smiled, pleased to be addressed as a boy. They began to wander round the farm, Timmy cross because he was on the lead. He pulled at it, wanting to run round and explore on his own. But George wouldn't let him. 'Not till you've made friends with all the other dogs,' she said. 'I wonder where they are?'

'Must have gone out with Morgan,' said Dick. 'Come on – let's go and look at the cows in the sheds. I do love the smell of cows.'

They wandered round the farm, enjoying the pale sun, the keen wind, and the feeling that their legs belonged to them at last, and were not likely to give way at any moment. They hardly coughed at all, and felt quite annoyed when one or other suddenly began.

'I shall let old Timmy off the lead a bit now,' said George. 'I can't see a dog about anywhere.' So she slipped the lead off his collar and he ran off joyfully at once, sniffing here, there and everywhere. He disappeared round a corner, his tongue hanging out happily.

And then the most appalling barking began! The children stopped as if they had been shot. It wasn't one dog, or even two – it sounded like a dozen! The four rushed round the corner of a barn at once – and there was poor Timmy, standing with his back to the barn, growling and barking and snarling at three fierce dogs!

'No, George, no, don't go to Timmy,' shouted Julian, seeing that George was going to rescue Tim, whatever happened. 'Those dogs are savage!'

But what did George care for that? She raced to Timmy, stood in front of him, and yelled at the three surprised dogs snarling there. 'HOW DARE YOU! GET AWAY! GO HOME! I SAID GO HOME!'

5 Things might be worse!

The three snarling dogs took no notice of George. It was Timmy they wanted. Who was this strange dog who dared to come wandering round their home? They tried to get at him, but George stood there, swinging the leather lead, and giving first one dog and then another a sharp flick. Julian rushed to help her – and then Timmy gave a sharp yelp. He had been bitten!

Someone came rushing round the corner. It was Mrs Jones, running as if she were a twelve-year-old!

'Tang! Bob! Dai!' she called, but the three dogs took no notice of her. And then, from somewhere, came a voice. What a voice! It echoed all round the farmyard as if it had come through a megaphone.

'DAI! BOB! TANG!'

And at the sound of that booming voice the three dogs stopped as if shot. Then they turned about and tore off at top speed.

'Thank God! That was Morgan,' panted the old woman, clutching her shawl round her. 'He must have heard the barking. Oh, my little dear – are you hurt?' She took hold of George's arm, and looked at her anxiously.

'I don't know. I don't think so,' said George, looking rather white. 'It's Timmy that's hurt. Oh, Tim, darling Tim, where did they bite you?'

'Woof!' said Timmy, who, though extremely

startled, didn't seem at all frightened. It had all happened so suddenly. George dropped down on her knees in the snow, and gave a little scream. 'He's been bitten on the neck – oh look! Poor, poor Timmy. *Why* did I let you off the lead?'

'It's not much, George,' said Julian, looking at the bleeding place. 'The other dog bit just where his collar is, look – and his teeth went through the collar, not really into Tim's neck. It's really not much more than a graze.'

Anne was leaning against the wall, looking sick, and Dick suddenly felt as if his legs were wobbly again. He couldn't help thinking what would have happened if the three savage dogs had bitten George instead of Timmy. Good old George! She was as brave as a lion!

'What a thing to happen!' said old Mrs Jones, upset. 'Why for did you let him loose my boy? You should have waited for my Morgan to come along with his dogs, and tell them your Timmy was a friend.'

'I know,' said George, still on her knees beside Timmy. 'It was all my fault. Oh, Timmy, I'm so thankful you've only got that one small bite. Mrs Jones, have you any TCP? I must put some on at once.'

But before Mrs Jones could answer, the giantlike figure of Morgan came round the corner of the barn, his three dogs, extremely subdued now, at his heels.

'Hey?' he said, inquiringly, looking at the four children and his mother.

'The dogs attacked this one,' explained his mother. 'You shouted just in time, Morgan. But he's not much hurt. You should have seen this boy here – the one the dog belongs to – he stood in front of his dog and fought off Tang, Bob and Dai!'

Julian couldn't help smiling to hear George continually called a boy – but, standing there in snow-trousers and coat, a woollen cap on her short hair, she looked very like a sturdy boy.

'Please come and get the TCP,' said George, anxiously, seeing a drop of blood drip from Timmy's neck on to the white snow. Morgan took a step forward and bent down to look at Timmy.

He made a small scornful sound and stood up again. '*He's* all right,' he said, and walked off.

George stared after him angrily. It was *his* dogs that had attacked and hurt Timmy – and he hadn't even been sorry about it! She felt so angry that tears came suddenly into her eyes. She blinked them away, ashamed.

'I don't think I want to stay here,' she said loudly, and clearly. 'Those dogs will be sure to attack Timmy again. They might kill him. I shall go home.'

'Now, now, you're just upset,' said kind old Mrs Jones, taking George's arm. George shook off her hand, scowling. 'I'm *not* upset. I'm just angry to think my dog should have been attacked for nothing – and I'm sure he'll be attacked again. And I want to see to his neck. I'm going indoors.'

She stalked off with Timmy at her heels, her head well up, bitterly ashamed of two more tears that suddenly ran down her cheeks. It wasn't like old George to cry! But she was still not quite herself after being ill. The other three looked at one another.

'Go with her, Anne,' said Julian, and Anne obediently ran after George. Julian turned to the worried old woman.

'You shouldn't stand out here in the cold,' he said, seeing that she was shivering, and pulling her shawl more closely round her. 'George will soon be all right. Don't take any notice of what she says.'

'*She!* What, isn't she a *boy*, then,' said Mrs Jones, in

surprise. But now, surely she won't go home, will she?'

'No,' said Julian, hoping he was right. You never could tell with George! 'She'll soon get over it. If we could get some TCP it would help, though! She's always terrified of wounds going bad, where Timmy is concerned.'

'Come away in, then,' said Mrs Jones, and hurried back to the farmhouse, refusing Julian's hand over the snow.

George was in the living room with Timmy. She had got some water and was bathing the wound with her handkerchief, having first taken off Tim's collar.

'I'll fetch you the TCP, boy,' said Mrs Jones, forgetting again that George was a girl. She ran to her kitchen, and came back with a big bottle of antiseptic. George took it gratefully, and dabbed some on Timmy, who stood still, quite enjoying all the fuss. He jumped a little when it stung him, and George patted him and praised him.

'He wouldn't mind having stuff dabbed on him all day long, George, if you would only make a fuss of him,' said Dick, with a laugh.

George looked up. 'He might have been killed,' she said. 'And if those dogs get him again, he certainly will be! I'm going to go back home – not to *your* home, Ju – but to my own, at Kirrin Cottage.'

'Oh, don't be silly, George,' said Dick, exasperated. 'Anyone would think Timmy had been injured for life or something. He's only got a skin wound! Why spoil what may be a jolly good holiday just for that?'

'I don't trust those three dogs,' said George, stubbornly. 'They'll be out to get Tim now – I know they will. I tell you I'm going home. I'm not spoiling *your* holiday – only my own.'

'Well, listen – stay one more day,' said Julian, hoping that if she did, George would see how stupidly she was behaving. 'Just *one* more day. That's not much to ask. It will upset old Mrs Jones dreadfully if you rush off like this – and it will be difficult to make arrangements for you to go back today, now that everywhere is under snow again.'

'All right,' said George, ungraciously. 'I'll stay till tomorrow. It will give Timmy a bit of time to get over his fright. But ONLY till tomorrow.'

'Tim's not frightened,' said Anne. 'George, he would have taken on all three dogs by himself if you hadn't gone to his help. Wouldn't you, Timmy?'

'Woof, woof!' said Timmy, agreeing at once. He wagged his tail vigorously. Dick laughed. 'Good old Tim!' he said. '*You* don't want to go home, do you?'

'Woof!' said Timmy, obligingly, and wagged his tail again. George put on one of her scowls, and Julian nudged the others to warn them to stop teasing her. He didn't want George suddenly to change her mind and rush off home straight away!

'I vote we go for a walk,' said Dick. 'It's a shame to stick indoors like this on this sunny, snowy day. Anne, are you coming?'

'I will if George does,' said Anne. But George shook her head.

'No,' she said. 'I'll stay in with Tim this morning. You go off together.'

Anne wouldn't come, so the boys left the two girls and went out into the keen, invigorating mountain air once more. Already they felt better, and were not coughing at all. What a pity this had happened! It spoilt things for everyone – even for old Mrs Jones, who now appeared at her front door, looking anxious.

'Don't you worry now, Mrs Jones,' said Julian. 'I

expect our cousin will be all right soon. She's given up the idea of rushing home today at any rate! My brother and I are going for a walk up the mountain. Which way is best?'

'Well now, take that path,' said the old woman, pointing. 'And go on till you come to our summer chalet. You can rest there before coming back – and if you don't want to come back for dinner, well, you'll find food in the cupboard there. Here is the key to get into the little place!'

'Oh thanks,' said Julian, surprised. That sounds good. We'd love to have our lunch up there, Mrs Jones – we'll be back before dark. Tell the girls for us, will you?'

And away they went, whistling. It was fun to have a day all to themselves, just the two of them, together!

They took the snowy path and began to climb up the slope of the mountain. The sun was now melting the snow a little, so they could make out the path fairly easily. Then they discovered that big black stones marked the way here and there – a guide to the farmer and his men, when the snow covered the path and everything!

The view was magnificent. As they climbed higher, they could see the tops of more and more hills, all of which sparkled snowy-white in the pale January sun. 'I *say* – if only we had a bit more snow, what tobogganing we could have down these slopes,' said Dick, longingly. 'I wish I'd brought my skis this morning – the snow is deep enough for them down that hill – we'd whizz along like lightning!'

They were glad when they at last came to the little hut or chalet that old Mrs Jones had spoken about. After two hours' climbing it was nice to think of having something to eat, and a good rest!

'It's quite a place,' said Julian, slipping the key into the lock. 'A little wooden house, with windows and all!'

He opened the door and went inside. Yes – it was a very fine little place indeed, with bunk beds let into the wooden walls, a stove for heating – and cupboards full of crockery – and tins of food! The two boys had the same idea at once, and swung round to one another.

'Couldn't we stay here – on our own? George would love it too,' said Julian, putting into words what Dick was already thinking. Oh – if only they *could*!

6 A funny little creature

The boys were tired, but not too tired to examine the little hut thoroughly – though it really was more like a one-roomed house. It faced across the deep valley, and the sun shone straight into it. Julian opened cupboard after cupboard, exclaiming in delight.

'Bedding! Towels! Crockery – and cutlery! And look at these tins of food – and bottles of orangeade and the rest! My word, people who come to stay at Magga Glen in the summer must have a fantastic time!'

'We could light the stove to heat the room,' suggested Dick, pulling the oil-stove into the middle of the room.

'No. We don't need to,' said Julian. 'The sun is pouring in, and it really isn't cold in here. We could wrap ourselves round in rugs from that cupboard if we want to.'

'Do you think we'd be allowed to come up here, instead of living down at the farm?' said Dick, opening a tin of ham with a tin-opener that hung on a nail by the cupboard. 'It's so *much* nicer to be quite on our own and independent! George would simply love it!'

'Well, we can *ask*,' said Julian, taking the cap off a bottle of orangeade. 'Can we find some biscuits to eat with this ham? Oh yes – here are some cream-cracker biscuits. I *say* – I'm really ravenous!'

'So am I,' said Dick, his mouth full. 'Pity George

was so silly – she and Anne could have enjoyed this too.'

'Well – perhaps on the whole it's as well they didn't come,' said Julian. 'I think Anne would have been too tired to come all this way on her first day – and George certainly had a worse cold and cough than anyone. A day at the farm will probably do her good. Gosh – she's absolutely fearless, isn't she? I'll never forget her standing up to those three savage dogs! I was jolly scared myself.'

'I'm going to get a rug and wrap it round me and sit out on the doorstep in the sun,' said Dick. 'That view is too marvellous for words!'

He and Julian took a rug each, and then sat out on the wooden doorstep, munching their ham and biscuits. They stared across at the great hill opposite.

'Is that a house on the slope over there – near the top, look,' said Dick, suddenly.

Julian stared across at the opposite hill, but could make out nothing.

'It can't be,' he said. 'The roof would be covered with snow, and we'd never see it. Besides, who would build a house so high up?'

'Plenty of people,' said Dick. 'It's not everyone who likes towns and shops and cinemas and traffic and the rest. I can imagine an artist building a house on one of these mountains, just for the view! He'd be quite happy looking at it and painting it all day long.'

'Well – I like a bit of company, I must say,' said Julian. 'This is all right for a week or two – but you'd need to be an artist or a poet – or a shepherd or something, to stand it all the time!'

He yawned. Both boys had finished their meal, and felt comfortably full and at peace. Dick yawned too, and lay back on his rug. But Julian pulled him upright.

'Oh no! We're not going to take naps up here! We'd sleep like logs again, and wake up in the dark. The sun's going down already, and we've got all that long walk back to the farm – and no torch to light our way if we go wrong!'

'There are those black stones,' said Dick, with another yawn. 'All right, all right – I agree with you! I certainly don't want to stumble down this mountain in the pitch dark!'

Julian suddenly clutched Dick's arm, and pointed upwards, where the path still wound on and on. Dick turned – and stared. Someone was up there, skipping down the path towards them, with a lamb gambolling around, and a small dog scampering after.

'Is it a boy or a girl?' said Julian, in wonder. 'My word – it must be cold, whichever it is!'

It was a small girl coming along, a wild-looking little creature with a mass of untidy black curls, a face as brown as an oak-apple – and very few clothes! She wore a dirty pair of boy's shorts, and a blue shirt. Her legs were bare, and she had old shoes on her feet. She was singing as she came, in a high sweet voice like a bird's.

The dog with her began to bark, and she stopped her song at once. She spoke to the dog, and he barked again, facing towards the hut. The lamb gambolled round without stopping.

The little girl looked towards the hut, and saw Julian and Dick. She turned at once and ran back the way she had come. Julian got up and shouted to her.

'It's all right! We shan't hurt you! Look – here's a bit of meat for your dog!'

The girl stopped and looked round, poised ready to run again at once. Julian waved the bit of ham left over from their meal. The little dog smelt it on the wind, and came running up eagerly. He snapped at it, got it into his mouth and ran back to the girl. He didn't attempt to eat it, but just stood there by her, looking up.

She bent down eagerly, and took it. She tore it in half and gave one piece to the eager dog, who swallowed it at once – and the other piece she ate herself, keeping a sharp eye on the two boys as she did so. The lamb came nosing round her, and she put one thin arm round its neck.

'What a funny little thing,' said Julian to Dick. 'Where *can* she have come from? She must be absolutely frozen!'

Dick called to the child.

'Hallo! Come and talk to us!'

She shot off at once as soon as he shouted. But she didn't go very far. She half hid behind a bush, peeping out now and again.

'Get some of those biscuits,' said Julian to Dick. 'We'll hold some out to her. She's like a wild thing.'

So Dick held out a handful of biscuits, and called:

'Bicuits! For you! And your dog!'

But only the lamb came gambolling up, a toy-like creature, with a tail that frisked and whisked all the time. It tried to get on to Dick's knee, and bumped its little black nose against his face.

'Fany, Fany!' called the small girl, in a high, clear voice. The lamb tried to get away but Dick held on to it. It seemed to be all legs!

'Come and get it!' shouted Dick. 'We shan't hurt you!'

The little girl couldn't bear to leave her lamb. She came out from the bush, and took a few hesitating steps towards the boys. The dog ran right up to them, snuffing at their hands for more ham. Julian gave him a biscuit and he crunched it up at once, giving sidelong glances at his watching mistress as if to apologise for eating it all himself? Julian patted the little thing and it licked him joyfully.

The little girl came nearer. Her legs looked blue with cold, but although she had so little on, she didn't seem to be shivering. Julian held out another biscuit. The dog jumped up and took it neatly in his mouth, running up to the little girl with it. The boys burst into laughter, and the small girl smiled suddenly, her whole face lighting up.

'Come here!' called Julian. 'Come and get your pretty lamb. We've got some more biscuits for you and your dog.'

At last the child came near to them, as watchful as a hare, ready to turn at a moment's notice. The boys sat still and patient, and soon the girl was near enough to snatch a biscuit and retreat again. She sat down on one of the black stones marking the path, and munched her biscuit, staring at them all the time out of her big dark eyes.

'What's your name?' asked Dick, not moving from his place, afraid that the child would leap off like a frightened goat.

The girl didn't seem to understand. Dick repeated his question, speaking slowly.

'What – is – your – name? What – are – you – called?'

The child nodded her head and then pointed to herself.

'Me – Aily,' she said.

She pointed at the dog.

'Dai,' she said, and he leapt up at his name and covered her with licks. Then she pointed to the lamb, which was now gambolling round the boys like a mad thing. 'Fany,' she said.

'Ah – Aily – Dai – Fany,' said Julian, solemnly, and he too pointed at first one then the other. Then he pointed to himself. 'Julian!' he said, and then pointed to Dick. 'Dick!'

The little girl gave a high, clear laugh, and suddenly poured out quite a long speech. The boys couldn't understand a word of it.

'She's speaking in Welsh, I suppose,' said Dick, disappointed. 'What a pity – it sounds lovely, but I can't make head or tail of it.'

The child saw that they had not understood. She frowned, as if thinking hard.

'My da – he up high – sheep!' she said.

'Oh – your father's a shepherd up there!' said Dick. 'But you don't live with him, do you?'

Aily considered this, then shook her head.

'Down!' she said, pointing. 'Aily down!' Then she turned to the dog and the lamb, and cuddled them both. 'Dai mine,' she said, proudly. 'Fany mine!'

'Nice dog. Nice lamb,' said Julian, solemnly, and the little girl nodded in delight. Then, for no reason that the boys could see, she stood up, leapt down the hill, followed by the lamb and the dog, and disappeared.

'What a funny little creature!' said Dick. 'Like a pixie of the hills, or an elf of the woods. I quite expected her to disappear in smoke, or something. I should think she runs completely wild, wouldn't you? We'll ask Mrs Jones about her when we get back!'

'My goodness – come on, the sun's getting quite low,' said Julian, getting up in a hurry. 'We've got to put the things away, and fold up the rugs, and lock up. Buck up – once the sun goes it will be dark almost at once, and we've quite a long way to go.'

It didn't take them long to tidy up and lock the little

house carefully. Then down the path they went at top speed. The sun had melted most of the snow farther down, and the going was easy. The boys felt exhilarated by their day on the mountainside and sang as they went, until they were quite out of breath.

'There's the farmhouse,' said Dick, and both boys were glad to see it. Their legs were tired now, and they longed for a good meal and a rest in a warm room.

'I hope George has recovered a bit by now – and is *still* at the farm!' said Julian, with a laugh. 'You never know with old George! I hope she'll like the sound of that hut. We'll ask Mrs Jones about it tonight, when we've talked it over with Anne and George.'

'Here we are,' said Dick, thankfully, as they went up to the house. 'Anne! George! We're back – where are you?'

7 Back at the farm again

Anne came running to meet Dick and Julian.

'Oh, I'm glad you're back!' she said. 'It's beginning to get dark, and I was afraid you'd lose your way!'

'Hallo, George!' said Julian, seeing her behind Anne, in the darkness of the passage. 'How's Timmy?'

'All right, thank you,' said George, sounding quite cheerful. 'Here he is!'

Timmy barked loudly and jumped up at the boys in welcome. He was very glad to see them, for he had been afraid that they had gone back home. They all went into the living room, where there was an enormous wood fire, looking very cheerful indeed. Julian and Dick fell into the two most comfortable chairs and spread their legs out to the fire.

'Ha! This is good!' said Dick. 'I couldn't have walked another step. I don't believe I can even go up the stairs to wash. We've walked MILES!'

They told the girls about their day, and when they described the little summer chalet, the two girls listened eagerly.

'Oh – I wish we'd gone with you,' said Anne, longingly. 'Timmy would have been quite all right, wouldn't he, George? We've decided it's only a skin wound. Actually, you can hardly see it now.'

'But all the same, I'm going back home tomorrow,' said George, determinedly. 'I'm sorry I made such a fuss this morning – but *honestly* I thought Timmy had been badly bitten. Thank goodness he wasn't. Still, I'm not risking such a thing again. If I stay on here with him, he's sure to have those three dogs attacking him sometime or other, and he might be killed. I don't want to upset your holiday – but I can NOT stay on here with Tim.'

'All right, old thing,' said Julian, soothingly. 'Don't get so up-in-the-air about it. There – you've gone and started your cough again! Do you know, Dick and I haven't coughed once today!'

'Nor have I,' said Anne. 'The air is marvellous here. I think I ought to go back with George, though, Ju. She'd be miserable all by herself at home.'

'Listen,' said Julian. 'We've got an idea, Dick and I – one that means old George won't have to go home, and . . .'

'Nothing will make me stop here,' interrupted George at once. 'NOTHING!'

'Give me a chance to tell you what I've got up my sleeve,' protested Julian. 'It's about that mountain hut we've been to – Dick and I thought it would be a marvellous idea if we could all five of us go and spend our time there – instead of here. We'd be ABSO-LUTELY on our own then – the way we like to be!'

'Oh *yes*!' said Anne at once, delighted. They all three looked at George. She smiled suddenly.

'Yes – that *would* be fun. I'd like that. I don't suppose those dogs would come near there. And how heavenly to be on our own!'

'Mrs Jones said that her son Morgan told her we're going to have heavy falls of snow!' said Anne. 'We could spend all day long on those slopes with our toboggans and skis. Oh, George – what a pity Timmy can't ski! We'll have to leave him at the hut when we go off skiing!'

'Do you suppose Mrs Jones will mind us going off there?' said Dick.

'I don't think so,' said Anne. 'She was telling us today that parties of children go there alone in the summer, while their parents stay and have a peaceful time down here. I don't see why she shouldn't let us go. We'll ask her when she comes in with our high tea. I said we wouldn't have tea *and* supper – we'd just have one big meal. We didn't know what time you'd be back – and George and I had such an enormous dinner in the middle of the day that we knew we wouldn't want tea.'

'Yes. *I'd* rather have a big meal now, too,' said Julian, yawning widely. 'I'm afraid all I shall want to do afterwards is to go up to bed and fall asleep. I'm *marvellously* tired. In fact, I could go to sleep this very minute! I suppose you girls have been indoors all day long because of Timmy?'

'No. We took it in turns to go for a walk without him,' said Anne. 'George hasn't let him put his nose outside the door. Poor Timmy – he just couldn't understand it, and he whined and whined!'

'Never mind – he'll enjoy himself if we can go up to that hut,' said George, who was very cheerful indeed now. 'I *do* hope we can. It would be glorious fun.'

'Ju – come and wash,' said Dick, seeing that Julian had his eyes closed already. '*Julian!* Come and wash, I tell you – you don't want to miss your meal, do you?' Julian groaned and dragged himself up the stone stairway. But once he had sluiced himself in cold water he felt much better, and very hungry indeed. So did Dick.

'We didn't tell the girls about the funny little creature – what was her name now – Aily! And Dai her dog and Fany the lamb. We mustn't forget to ask Mrs Jones about them,' said Julian.

They went downstairs, feeling much fresher and were delighted to see that Mrs Jones had been in and laid the table. They went to see what there was for their high tea.

'Pork pie – home-made, of course,' said Dick. 'And what's this – golly, it's a cheese! How enormous! Smell it, Julian – it's enough to make you start eating straight away! And more of that home-made bread! Can't we start?'

'No – there are new-laid boiled eggs to begin with,' said Anne, with a laugh. 'And an apple pie and cream to end with. So I hope you really *are* hungry, you two!'

Mrs Jones came in with a pot of hot tea. She smiled at the boys as she set the big brown teapot down on the table. 'Have you had a nice day away up on the mountain?' she said. 'You look fine, both of you. Did you find the hut all right?'

'Yes, thank you,' said Julian. 'Mrs Jones, it's a marvellous hut. We . . .'

'Yes, yes – it's a good hut,' said Mrs Jones, 'and I was sorry that the two girls didn't go with you, such a fine day as it was, and the dog not really hurt! And to think that the girls want to go back home! I've been feeling sad about it all day.'

She really did seem hurt and grieved, and George looked very guilty. Julian patted Mrs Jones on the arm, and spoke comfortingly.

'Don't you worry about us, Mrs Jones. I've got a fine idea to tell you. What we'd *really* like is to go and live up at that hut, the five of us – then we'd be out of your way and Timmy would be out of the way of the farm dogs too! Do you think we might do that? Then

George wouldn't have to go home, as she had planned to do.'

'Well now! To go to that hut in this weather! What an idea!' said Mrs Jones. 'You'd be most uncomfortable, with no one to look after you, and see to your wants, and cook for you this cold weather. No, no . . .'

'We're used to looking after ourselves,' said Dick. 'We're awfully good at it, Mrs Jones. And, my word, the food you've got up there is enough to feed an army! And there are cups and plates and dishes – and knives and forks – and all kinds of bedding . . .'

'We'd have a *smashing* time,' said George, joining in eagerly. 'I don't really want to go home, Mrs Jones. It's so lovely in these mountains – and if the snow comes down, as your Morgan says, we'd be able to have winter sports all on our own!'

'Oh, do say it's all right,' begged Anne. 'We shall be quite safe and happy there – and we do promise to come down here again if we can't manage, or if anything goes wrong.'

'I'll see that things go all right,' said Julian, speaking in his most grown-up voice.

'Well – well, it's a funny idea,' said Mrs Jones, still taken aback. 'I'll have to talk to my Morgan about it first. Now sit you down and eat your meal. I'll get my Morgan to decide.'

She went out of the room, shaking her head, her mouth pursed up in disapproval. No fire! No hot meals! No one to 'manage' for them. What a dreadful time those children would have up in that hut in this weather!

The five set to work to demolish the good food on the table. George allowed Timmy to sit up on a chair too, and fed him with titbits for a treat. He was perfectly good and very well-mannered indeed.

'I almost expect him to hand me a plate of something!' said Anne, with a giggle. 'Tim, dear – do pass me the salt!'

Timmy put a paw on the table exactly as if he meant to obey Anne, and George hastily made him put it down again! What a meal that was! The pork pie was so good that everyone had two slices, as well as their boiled eggs. Then they started on the cheese, which even Timmy liked. There was very little room indeed for the apple pie that Mrs Jones brought in at the end!

'My goodness – I forgot that an apple pie was coming,' said Anne, in dismay, as the old woman walked in with a tray on which was a big apple pie and a jug of cream.

'Mrs Jones – when we were up at the hut, we saw such a funny little creature,' said Dick. 'She said her name was Aily and she had a lamb and . . .'

'Oh, Aily! That mad little thing!' said Mrs Jones, picking up the dirty plates. 'She's the shepherd's daughter – a little truant she is, runs off from school, and hides away in the hills with her dog and her lamb. She always has a lamb each year – it follows her about everywhere. They say there isn't a rabbit hole or a blackberry bush or a bird's nest that child doesn't know!'

'She was singing when we first saw her,' said Julian. 'Singing like a bird.'

'Ah, yes – she has a lovely voice,' said Mrs Jones. 'She's wild as a bird – there's nothing to be done with her. If she's scolded she goes off for weeks, no one knows where. Don't you let her come round that hut now, when you're there – she might steal from you!'

'Oh, yes – the hut! Have you spoken to Morgan about it?' said Dick, eagerly.

'Yes, I have indeed,' said Mrs Jones. 'And he says yes, to let you go. *He* doesn't want trouble with the dogs either. He says snow is coming for sure, but you'll be safe up there and you can all take your toboggans for there'll be a chance to use them! He'll help you up with your things.'

'Oh good! Thanks!' said Julian, and the others smiled and looked at one another joyfully. 'Thanks most awfully, Mrs Jones. We'll go tomorrow after breakfast!'

Tomorrow! After breakfast! Up to that lonely hut on the mountainside, just the Five of them together. What could be better than that?

8 Off to the little hut

Julian and Dick were so sleepy after their long day in the cold air, and their enormous meal, that they could not keep their eyes open for long.

'Go to bed, both of you!' said Anne, seeing them lying tired out in their chairs, when Mrs Jones had cleared away everything.

'Yes. I think we'd better,' said Julian, staggering up. 'Oh, my legs! They're stiff as sticks! Goodnight, you two girls, and Timmy. See you tomorrow – if we wake up!'

The two boys stumbled up the stone stairs to bed. George and Anne stayed downstairs, talking and reading. Timmy lay on the hearthrug, listening, his ears twitching towards Anne when she spoke, and then towards George as she answered. This little habit of his always made them laugh.

'It's *exactly* as if he was listening, but too lazy to join in our conversation!' said Anne. 'Oh, George – I really am glad you're not going home tomorrow. It would be the first time you'd ever done a thing like that! I'd just have *had* to come with you!'

'Don't let's talk about it,' said George. 'I feel rather ashamed of making such a fuss now. All the same I shall be terrified if I see any of those dogs again when I'm with Timmy. What a bit of luck the boys went up to that hut today, Anne – we'd never have known about it if they hadn't.'

'Yes. It sounds fun,' said Anne. 'Don't let's be too late to bed, George. It will be quite a pull up the mountainside tomorrow, with all our things!'

George went to the window.

'It's snowing hard,' she said. 'Just as Morgan said it would. I don't like him, do you?'

'Oh – I think he's all right,' said Anne. 'And what a voice he's got! He nearly made me jump out of my skin when he called his three dogs. He must have the loudest voice in the world!'

'Timmy – you're yawning!' said George, as Timmy opened his mouth widely and made a yawning noise. 'How's your neck?'

Timmy was getting rather tired of having his neck examined. He lay still while George had another look at it.

'Healing beautifully!' she said. 'You'll be quite all right tomorrow. Will you like going off to that hut all by ourselves, Tim?'

Timmy gave her a loving lick and yawned again. Then he got up and trotted over to the door that led to the stone stairs, looking back inquiringly at George.

'Right. We're coming,' said George, laughing, and she and Anne blew out the lamp on the table, and followed Timmy up the stairs. They peeped in at the boys' room – and saw Julian and Dick absolutely sound asleep, dead to the world!

'A thunderstorm wouldn't wake them tonight!' said Anne. 'Come on – let's buck up and get into bed ourselves. We've a nice wood fire again, and I shall undress in front of it. Move over, Timmy. I want to stand on the rug.'

In the morning the world was very white indeed! As Morgan had prophesied, the snow had fallen thickly in the night, and everywhere was covered in a thick

white blanket, that gleamed and sparkled in the weak
January sun.

'This is something like it!' said Dick, as he looked
out of his bedroom. 'Get up, Ju – it's a marvellous
morning! Remember, we've got to take all our things
up to that hut today! Do stir yourself!'

Mrs Jones gave them a fine breakfast – eggs, bacon
and sausages.

'It's the last hot meal you'll have, if you're going up
to that hut,' she said. 'Though you'll be able to cook
eggs in the little saucepan up there, if you set it on top
of the oil-stove. And mind you don't get playing
about round that stove when it's alight, or the whole
place might go up in flames!'

'We'll be very careful,' promised Julian. 'I'll send
anyone back if they upset the stove – yes, I will, so just
look out, Timmy!'

'Woof!' said Tim, amiably. He was pleasantly excited with all the preparations for going, and ran
sniffing from one parcel to another.

The children were not taking all their things, of
course, but Mrs Jones had made them pack a complete
change of clothes each, besides their warmest night-
clothes and dressing-gowns. They had torches too,
and plenty of rope for hauling things up and down the
hills. And also they had six loaves of new-baked bread,
a large cheese, about three dozen eggs and a ham. So
they were truly well provided for.

'And there's plenty of butter packed in with the
loaves,' said Mrs Jones, 'and a large pot of cream. I'll
try and send up some milk if the shepherd comes
down. He'll pass the hut when he goes up again.
There's only a quart in the bottle there – but you'll find
plenty of orangeade and lemonade in the hut – and you
can boil snow if you want to make cocoa or tea!'

It was quite clear that Mrs Jones had no idea how many times the Five had gone off on their own! They smiled and winked at one another, and took all her advice in good part. She really was so kind, so very concerned about them all. She even packed some bones and dog biscuits for Timmy!

'Here's my Morgan now,' said Mrs Jones, when every single thing had been put in a pile outside the front door, toboggans and skis as well. 'He's brought his snow-slide with him, to take all your goods.'

The snow-slide was like a long flat cart with runners instead of wheels – an elongated sleigh. The children piled on to it all the parcels and two suitcases. They were all going to walk up as the snow was not yet too thick. Timmy danced round in great excitement – though both he and George kept a wary eye out for the other dogs, and Timmy did not venture very far from George.

The giantlike Morgan arrived, his breath puffing before him like a smoke-cloud! He nodded at the children.

'Morning,' he said, and that was all. He took hold of the ropes at the front of the snow-slide and ran them over his shoulders.

'I'll take one,' said Julian. 'It's much too heavy for one person to pull!'

'Ha!' said Morgan, scornfully, and walked off with the two ropes over his shoulder. The snow-slide followed easily.

'Strong as a horse, is my Morgan,' said old Mrs Jones, proudly.

'Strong as *ten* horses!' said Julian, wishing he was as big and as strong as the broad-shouldered farmer.

George said nothing. She hadn't yet forgiven the farmer for being scornful about Timmy's bite the day before. She followed the others, carrying her skis, and waved to kind old Mrs Jones as she stood anxiously watching them leave.

It seemed a long trek up the mountainside, when things had to be pulled or carried! Morgan went first, pulling the big snow-slide easily. Julian went next, pulling a toboggan and carrying his skis. Dick was next with another toboggan and skis, and the girls came last with their skis only. Timmy ran at the front or the back as he liked, enjoying everything.

Morgan said nothing at all. Julian addressed a few polite remarks to him, and received a grunt in reply, but that was all. He looked curiously at the great, strong fellow, wondering about him and his silence. He *looked* intelligent and even kindly – but he seemed so dour and rough in his manners and behaviour! Oh well – they would soon say goodbye to him and be on their own!

They came at last to the little hut. The girls ran ahead to it, exclaiming in delight. George looked through the windows.

'Oh – it's a proper little house inside! Oh, look at those bunks on the walls! And there's even a carpet on the floor! Quick, Julian, where's the key?'

'Morgan's got it,' said Julian, and they all stood by and waited while Morgan unlocked the door for them.

'Thanks so much for helping to bring up our things,' said Julian, politely. 'It was very kind of you.'

Morgan grunted, but looked pleased.

'Shepherd comes by at times,' he said, in his great deep voice, and the Five felt quite surprised to hear him saying even a short sentence to them! 'He'll take messages for you if you want.'

And with that he set off down the hill back to the

farm, with enormous swinging steps, like a giant from an old-time tale.

'He's peculiar,' said Anne, looking after him. 'I don't know if I like him or not.'

'What does it matter?' said Dick. 'Come on, Anne, old girl, give a hand. There's plenty to do. What about you and George seeing what blankets and things are in those cupboards, so we can make up some beds for tonight.'

Anne loved that kind of thing, though George didn't. She would much rather have carried in the things. But she went to the cupboards with Anne, and examined all their contents with much interest.

'Plenty of rugs and blankets and pillows,' said Anne. 'And enough china and cutlery for half a dozen families too! I suppose old Mrs Jones has dozens of people here in the summer! George, I'll put the food away, if you'll see to the beds.'

'Right,' said George, and went to make up four of the bunk beds. There were six of these altogether, in rows of three – three on one wall, three on another, one above the other. George was soon struggling with blankets and pillows, while Anne set out the food they had brought with them, arranging it neatly on the cupboard shelves. Then she went to look at the stove to see if it had oil in it, for it would be very cold that night.

'Yes, it's full,' she said. 'I'll light it tonight, because I expect we'll be out as long as it's daylight, won't we, Dick?'

'You bet!' said Dick, unpacking some of the things out of his suitcase. 'By the way, there's a little wooden bunker outside, with a can of extra oil and an enamel jug. I suppose the jug's for fetching water from some spring or other in the summertime – but we can easily melt snow for water. Will you two girls be long, Anne?'

'No. We've almost finished,' said Anne. 'Do you want something to eat before we go? Or shall we take some bread and ham with us, and have a good meal when we come back?'

'Oh, take some sandwiches,' said Julian. 'I don't want to stop for a meal. Besides, we can't be hungry yet. Let's make sandwiches – and we'll take some of those apples with us too!'

The sandwiches were quickly made, and the boys filled their pockets with apples. Timmy danced round in delight.

'You won't be quite so pleased, Tim, when you find yourself in *deep* snow!' said Dick. 'I wonder if he'll like travelling down the hill on a toboggan, George!'

'Oh, he'll love it!' said George. 'Won't you, Tim? Are we ready? Well, lock the door, Ju, and off we go!'

9 A strange tale

The children did not bother about their skis that first day. For one thing the snow was not quite thick or smooth enough for skiing, and for another thing they longed for the swift excitement of tobogganing. Dick took George on his toboggan and Julian took Anne on his. Timmy wouldn't come on either of them.

'Race you to the bottom!' Julian shouted. 'One, two, three, go!' And away they went, swishing over the clean white snow at top speed, shouting with laughter.

Julian won easily, because Dick's toboggan caught on a root or small bush under the snow, which upset it very suddenly. Dick and George were flung headlong into the snow, and sat up, blinking, and spitting out the cold snow from their mouths.

Timmy was terribly excited. He came plunging down the hillside after the toboggans, annoyed at the way his legs went into the snow, barking madly. He was most astonished to see Dick and George fly into the air when their toboggan upset, and pranced round them, licking them and leaping on them in a most aggravating way.

'Oh, *get* away, Timmy!' said Dick, trying to get up, and being knocked down again by the excited dog. 'Go and knock George over, not me! Call him, George!'

Pulling the toboggans back up the hill was a tiring

job – but the swift flight down over the snow was
worth all the pullings-up! The four children soon had
glowing faces and tingling limbs, and wished they
could throw off their coats and scarves!

'I can't pull up our toboggan one more time!' said
Anne, at last. 'I really can't. You'll have to pull it up
yourself, Julian, if you want to toboggan any more.'

'Well, I do want to – but my legs will hardly walk up
the hill now,' said Julian, panting. 'Hey, Dick – Anne
and I have had enough. We'll go up and eat our
sandwiches at the top of the slope, where we can watch
you.'

The other two soon joined them, and Timmy was
glad to sit down too. His long pink tongue hung out of
his mouth, and he puffed his white breath out like
rolling mist! At first he had been puzzled by what he
thought was 'smoke' coming out of his mouth so
continually, but now, seeing that everyone was apparently puffing it out too, he didn't worry!

The Five sat at the top of the slope, eating their
sandwiches hungrily, very glad of the rest. Julian
grinned round at them all.

'Pity Mother can't see us now!' he said. 'We look
marvellous! And nobody's coughed once. I bet we'll
be stiff tomorrow though!'

Dick was looking across the slope to the opposite
hill, rising steeply up a mile or so away.

'*There's* that building I thought I saw yesterday,' he
said. 'Isn't that a chimney sticking up?'

'You've got sharp eyes!' said George. 'Nobody
could surely see a building as far away as that, when
the snow is on it!'

'Did we bring the field-glasses?' asked Julian.
'Where are they? We could soon find out if there's a
house there or not, if we look through those.'

'I put them into a cupboard,' said Anne, getting up. 'Ooooh, I'm stiff! I'll just go and get them.'

She soon came back with the glasses and handed them to Dick. He put them to his eyes and adjusted them, till they were properly focused on the faraway hill opposite.

'Yes,' he said. 'I was right. It *is* a building – and I'm pretty sure it must be Old Towers, too. You know – the place we went to by mistake two nights ago when we lost our way.'

'Let's have a look,' said Anne. 'I think I might recognise it. I caught a glimpse of the towers when we swung round a corner on the way up Old Towers Hill.' She put the glasses to her eyes and gazed through them.

'Yes. I'm sure that's the place,' she said. 'Wasn't it odd – that big rude notice on the gate – and that fiercely barking dog – and nobody about! How lonely the old lady must be living there all by herself!'

As they sat there, nibbling their apples, Timmy suddenly began to bark. He stood up, turning his head towards the path that ran higher up the hill.

'Perhaps it's Aily, that funny child, coming,' said Julian, hopefully. But it wasn't. It was a small, wiry-looking woman, a shawl over her head, neatly dressed, walking swiftly.

She didn't seem very surprised to see the children. She stopped and said 'Good day'.

'You'll be the boys my Aily was telling me of last night,' she said. 'Are you staying in the Jones's hut?'

'Yes,' said Julian. 'We were staying at the farm first – but our dog didn't get on with the others, so we've come up here. It's fine. Marvellous view, too!'

'If you see that Aily of mine, tell her not to stay out

tonight,' said the woman, wrapping her shawl more tightly round her. 'Her and her lamb! She's as mad as the old lady in the house over there!' and she pointed in the direction of Old Towers.

'Oh – do you know anything about that old place?' asked Julian, at once. 'We went to it by mistake, and . . .'

'Well, you didn't get into it, I'll be bound,' said Aily's mother. 'Notices on the gate and all! And to think I used to go up there three times a week, and never anything but kindness shown me! And now old Mrs Thomas, she won't see a soul except those friends of her son's. Poor old lady – she's out of her mind, so they say. Must be – or she'd see me, who worked for her for years!'

This was all very interesting.

'Why do they say "Keep out" on the gates?' asked Julian. 'They've a fierce dog there, too.'

'Ah well, young man, you see some of the old lady's friends would like to know what's going on,' said Aily's mother. 'But nobody can do a thing. It's a strange place now – with noises at night – and mists – and shimmerings – and . . .'

Julian began to think that was an old wives' tale, made up because the villagers were angry that they were now kept out of the big old house. He smiled.

'Oh, you may smile, young man,' said the woman, sounding cross. 'But ever since last October, there have been strange goings on there. And what's more, vans have been there in the dead of night. What for, I'd like to know? Well, if you ask me, I reckon they've been taking away the poor old thing's belongings – furniture and pictures and such. Poor Mrs Thomas – she was sweet and kind, and now I don't know what's happened to her!'

There were tears in the woman's eyes, and she hastily brushed them away.

'I shouldn't be telling you all this – you'll be scared sleeping here alone at night now.'

'No – no, we shan't,' Julian assured her, amused that she should think that a village tale might frighten them. 'Tell us about Aily. Isn't she frozen, going about with so few clothes on?'

'That child! She's a one, I tell you,' said Aily's mother. 'Runs about the hills like a wild thing – plays truant from school – goes to see her father – he's a shepherd, up there where the sheep are – and doesn't come home at nights. You tell her there's a good scolding waiting for her at home if she doesn't come back tonight. She's like her father, she is – likes to be alone all the time – talks to the lambs and the dogs as if they were human – but never a word to me!'

The children began to feel uncomfortable, and wished they hadn't spoken to the grumbling gossipy woman. Julian got up.

'Well – if we see Aily, we'll certainly tell her to go home – but not about the scolding, because I expect she *wouldn't* go home then,' he said. 'If you pass by the farmhouse will you be kind enough to step in and tell Mrs Jones we are quite all right, and enjoying ourselves very much? Thank you!'

The woman nodded her head, muttered something, and went off down the hill, walking as swiftly as before.

'She said some funny things,' said Dick, staring after her. 'Was that a silly village tale she told us – or do you suppose there's something in it, Ju?'

'Oh – a village tale of course!' said Julian, sensing that Anne hadn't liked it much. 'What a strange family – a shepherd who spends all his time on the hills – a child who wanders about the countryside with a lamb and a dog – and a mother who stops and tells such angry tales to strangers!'

'It's getting dark,' said Dick. 'I vote we go in and light the oil–stove and get the hut warm – and light the table lamp too. It'll be cosy in there. I'm feeling a bit chilled now, sitting out here so long.'

'Well, don't begin to cough,' said Julian, 'or you'll set us all off! Indoors, Tim! Come on!'

Soon they were all in the hut, the oil–stove giving out a lovely warmth and glow, and the table lamp shining brightly.

'We'll play a game, shall we?' said Dick. 'And have a sort of high tea later. Let's have a *silly* game – snap, or something!'

So they sat down to play – and soon Dick's cards had all been 'snapped' by the others. He yawned and went to the window, looking out into the darkness that hid all the snowy hills. Then he stood tense for a moment, staring in surprise. He spoke to the others without turning.

'Quick! Come here, all of you! Tell me what you make of *this*! Did you ever see such an extraordinary thing! QUICK!'

10 *In the middle of the night*

'What is it, Dick? What can you see?' cried George, putting down her cards as soon as she heard Dick's call. Julian rushed to stand beside him at once, imagining all sorts of things. Anne went too, with Timmy leaping excitedly. They all stared out of the window, Anne half afraid.

'It's gone!' cried Dick, in disappointment.

'But what *was* it?' asked George.

'I don't know. It was over there – on the opposite slope, where Old Towers is,' said Dick. 'I don't know how to describe it – it was like a – like a rainbow – no, not quite like that – how *can* I describe it?'

'Try,' said Julian, excited.

'Well – let me think – you know how, on a very hot day, all the air *shimmers*, don't you?' said Dick. 'Well, that's what I saw on the hill over there – rising high into the sky and then disappearing. A shimmering!'

'What colour?' asked Anne, amazed.

'I don't know – all colours it seemed,' said Dick. 'I don't quite know how to explain – it's something I've never seen before. It just came suddenly – and the shimmering rose all the way up into the sky, and then disappeared. That's all.'

'Well – that's what Aily's mother said – mists – and shimmerings,' said Julian, remembering. 'Gosh – so that *wasn't* just a tale she told us. There was some truth in it. But what in the wide world can this shimmering be?'

'Had we better go back to the farm and tell them there?' asked Anne, hopefully, not at all wanting to spend the night in the hut now.

'No! They've probably heard the tale already,' said Julian. 'Besides – this is exciting. We might be able to find out something more about it. We can easily watch Old Towers from here – it's one of the very few places where anyone can look straight across at it. As the crow flies, it's less than a mile away – though it's many miles by road.'

They all gazed towards the opposite hill again, though they couldn't see it, of course, hoping something would happen. But nothing did happen. The sky was pitch black, for heavy clouds had come up – and the distant hill couldn't be seen.

'Well – I'm tired of looking out in the darkness,' said Anne, turning away. 'Let's get on with our game.'

'Right,' said Julian, and they all sat down again, Dick watching the others play, but occasionally glancing out of the window into the black darkness there.

Anne was out of the game next, and she got up and went to the food cupboard.

'I think I'll start preparing a meal,' she said. 'We'll have boiled eggs, shall we, to begin with – and I'll boil a kettle too and make some cocoa – or would you rather have tea?'

'Cocoa,' said everyone, and Anne got out the tin.

'I'll want some snow, for the kettle,' she said.

'Well, there's some nice clean snow just behind the hut,' said Dick. 'Oh wait, Anne – you won't like going out in the dark now, will you? I'll get it! If you hear me yell, you'll know there's something going on!'

Timmy went out with him, much to Anne's relief.
She held the kettle, waiting for the snow – and then
suddenly there came a loud yell!

'Hey! Who's that?'

Anne let go the kettle in fright, and it dropped on
the floor with a crash, making the other two jump
violently. Julian rushed to the door.

'Dick! What's up?'

Dick appeared at the doorway, grinning, with
Timmy beside him.

'Nothing much. Sorry if I frightened you. But I was
just scraping up some snow in the basin here, when
something rushed at me, and butted me!'

'Whatever was it?' said George, startled. 'And why
didn't Timmy bark?'

'Because he knew it was harmless, I suppose,' said
Dick, grinning aggravatingly. 'Here, Anne – here's
the snow for the kettle.'

'*Dick!* Don't be so annoying!' said George. 'Who
was out there?'

'Well – I couldn't really see much, because I'd put
my torch down to scrape up the snow,' said Dick. 'But
I rather *think* it was Fany the lamb! It was gone before I
had time to call out. I got quite a shock!'

'Fany the lamb!' said Julian. 'Well – that must mean
that little Aily is about. What *can* she be doing out in
the darkness at this time of night?'

He went to the door and called:

'Aily! Aily, if you're there, come in here and we'll
give you something to eat.'

But there was no answering call. Nobody appeared
out of the darkness, no lamb came frisking up.

Timmy stood by Julian, looking out into the darkness, his ears pricked. He had been surprised when the
tiny lamb trotted up out of the darkness, and had had

half a mind to bark. But who would bark at a lamb?
Not Timmy!

Julian shut the door.

'If that kid is out there on this frosty night, with only
the few clothes she had on yesterday, I should think
she'll catch her death of cold,' he said. 'Cheer up, Anne
– and for goodness' sake, don't be scared if you hear a
noise outside or see a little face looking in at the
window. It will only be that mad little Aily!'

'I don't want to see *any* faces looking in at the
window, whether it's Aily or not,' said Anne, putting
snow into the kettle. 'Honestly I think she *must* be
mad, wandering about these snowy hills alone at
night. I don't wonder her mother was cross.'

It wasn't long before they were all sitting round the
small table eating a very nice meal. Boiled eggs, laid
that morning, cheese and new bread and butter, and a
jar of home-made jam they found in the cupboard.
They drank steaming hot cups of cocoa, into each of
which Anne had ladled a spoonful of cream.

'No King or Queen in all the world could possibly
have enjoyed their meal more than I have,' said Dick.
'Anne, shall I take the milk and cream out into the
snow – they'll keep for ages out there.'

'All right. But for goodness' sake don't put them
where the lamb can get them – if it *was* a lamb that
butted you,' said Anne, giving them to Dick. 'And
don't yell again if you can help it!'

However, Dick didn't see anything this time, nor
did anything come up and butt him. He was quite
disappointed!

'I'll wash the plates and cups out in the snow tomorrow,' said Anne. 'How long are you all going to stay
up? It's awfully early, I know – but I'm half asleep
already! The air up here is so very strong!'

'All right. We'll all pack up,' said Julian. 'You take those two bunks over there, girls, and we'll have these. Shall we have the little oil-stove on, or not?'

'Yes,' said Dick. 'This place will be an ice-box if we don't!'

'I'd like it on too,' said Anne. 'What with shimmerings and buttings and yellings I feel I'd like a little light in the room, even if it only comes from an oil-stove!'

'Well – I know you don't believe my "shimmerings",' said Dick. 'But I swear they're true! And what's more, I bet we'll all see them before we leave this hut! Well – good night, girls – I'm for bed!'

In a few minutes' time the bunks were creaking as the four children settled into them. They were not as comfortable as beds, but quite good. George's bunk creaked more than anyone's.

'I suppose you've got *Timmy* in your bunk, making it creak like that!' said Anne sleepily. 'Well, I'm glad I'm in the bunk *above* yours, George. I bet Tim falls out in the night!'

One by one they fell asleep. The oil-stove burned steadily. It was turned rather low, and shadows quivered on the ceiling and walls. And then something made Timmy's ears prick up as he lay asleep on George's feet. First one ear pricked up – and then the other – and suddenly. Timmy sat up straight and growled in his throat. Nobody awoke – they were all too sound asleep.

Timmy growled again and again – and then he barked sharply. 'WOOF!'

Everyone awoke at once. Timmy barked again, and George put out a hand to him.

'Sh! What's the matter? Is there someone about, Tim?'

'What's up, do you think?' said Julian, from his

bunk on the other side of the room. Nobody could
hear or see anything out of the ordinary. Why was
Timmy barking, then?

The oil-stove was still burning, its light throwing a
small round pattern of yellow on the ceiling. It made a
small cosy noise as it burned, a kind of bubbling.
There was nothing else to be heard at all.

'It must be someone prowling outside,' said Dick at
last. 'Shall we let Timmy go and see?'

'Well – let's lie down and see if he barks again,' said
Julian. 'For all we know a mouse may have run across
the floor. Tim would bark at that just as soon as he
would bark at an elephant!'

'Yes. You're right,' said George. 'All right – we'll
lie down again. Timmy's lying down too. Now, for
goodness sake, Tim, if it is a mouse somewhere, do
use your common sense, and let it play if it wants to
– and don't wake us up.'

Timmy licked her face. He kept his ears well up for a
while. The others all went to sleep except Anne. She
lay with her eyes open, wondering what had startled
Timmy. She didn't believe it was a mouse!

So it was the wakeful Anne who heard the noise
when it came again. She thought at first that it was just
a noise in her ears, the kind she often heard when she
lay down to sleep, and the room was quiet. But then
she felt certain that it *wasn't* in her ears – it was a *real*
noise. But what a peculiar one!

'It's a kind of deep, deep, grumbling noise,' thought
Anne, sitting up. Timmy gave a little whine as if to say
he was hearing something again too. 'A sort of
thunder-rumble, but far below me, not above!'

It grew a little louder, and Timmy growled.

'It's all right, Tim,' whispered Anne. 'It *must* be far-
off thunder, I think!'

But then the shuddering began! This was so astonishing that Anne didn't know what to make of it. At first she thought it was herself, beginning to shiver with the cold. But no – even her bunk vibrated to her fingers when she touched the wooden side!

Then she really *was* frightened. She called out loudly.

'Julian! Dick! Wake up – something odd is happening. Do wake up!'

And Timmy began to bark again. Woof, woof, woof! WOOF, WOOF!

11   *Strange happenings*

Everyone awoke at Anne's call. Julian thought he was in bed, and leapt out, forgetting that he was in the top bunk. He landed with a crash on the floor, shaken and alarmed.

'Oh, Ju! You forgot you were in the top bunk!' said George, half scared and half amused. 'Are you hurt? Anne, whatever is the matter? Why did you call out? Did you see something?'

'No. I *heard* something – and *felt* something!' said Anne, glad that the others were awake. 'So did Timmy. But it's all gone now.'

'Yes, but what *was* it?' asked Julian, sitting on the edge of Dick's bunk, and rubbing his knee, which had struck the floor when he fell.

'It was a . . . a . . . well . . . a kind of very very deep *rumbling*,' said Anne. 'A *deep-down* rumbling – very far away. Not like thunder up in the sky. More like a thunderstorm underground! And then there was a . . . *shuddering*! I felt the edge of my bunk and it seemed to be sort of – well – *quivering*. I can't quite explain it. I was awfully scared.'

'Sounds like a small earthquake,' said Dick, wondering if Anne had dreamt all this. 'Anyway – you can't hear or feel it now, can you? You're sure you didn't dream all this, Anne?'

'*Quite* sure!' said Anne, 'I . . .' And just at that very moment it all began again! First the curious grumbling, muffled, and 'deep-down', as Anne had described it – then the equally strange 'shuddering'. It crept through their bodies till they were all shuddering a little too, and could not stop.

'It's as if we were shivering in every part of us,' said Dick, in wonder. 'Sort of vibrating as if we had tiny dynamo engines working inside us.'

'Yes! You've described it exactly!' said George. 'Goodness – when I put my hand on Timmy I can *feel* him doing the "shudders" – and it's just like putting my hand on something working by electricity! You know the sort of small vibrations you feel then.'

'It's gone!' said Dick, just as George finished speaking. 'I'm not "shuddering" any more. It suddenly stopped. And I can't hear that grumbling, far-off noise now. Can you?'

Everyone agreed that both the noise and the shuddering had stopped. What in the wide world could it be?

'It must be something to do with that curious "shimmering" I saw in the sky over Old Towers Hill tonight,' said Dick, remembering. 'I've a good mind to go and look out of the window that faces the hill opposite, and see if it's there again.'

He leapt out of his bunk and ran to the window. At once he gave a loud cry. 'Come and look! Whew! Just come and look!'

All the others, Timmy as well, rushed to the window at once, Timmy standing on his hind legs to see. Certainly there was something weird to look at!

Over the hill opposite hung a mist – a curious glowing mist, that stood out in the pitch black darkness of the night! It swirled heavily, not lightly as a mist usually does.

'Look at that!' said Anne, in wonder. 'What a

strange colour – not red – not yellow – not orange. What colour *is* it?'

'It's not a shade I've ever seen before,' said Julian, rather solemnly. 'I call this jolly strange. What's *happening* here? No wonder Aily's mother told us those stories – there's really something in them! We'd better make a few inquiries tomorrow.'

'It's funny that both the shimmering I saw and that cloud too are over Old Towers Hill,' said Dick. 'You don't think it's something that's happening in Old Towers House, do you?'

'No. Of course not,' said Julian. 'What could happen there that would make us feel the effects here, in this hut – that strange shuddering, for instance? And how in the world could we hear a rumbling from a mile or so away, if it were not thunder? And that certainly wasn't.'

'The mist is going,' said Anne. 'Look – it's changing colour – no, it's just going darker. It's gone!'

They stood looking out for a while longer, and then Julian felt Anne shivering violently beside him.

'You're frozen!' he said. 'Come on, back to bed. You don't want to get another awful cold and cough. My word – this is all very peculiar. But I expect there's a sensible explanation – probably there are mines around here, and work is being done at night as well as day.'

'We'll find out,' said Dick, and they all climbed thankfully back into their bunks, feeling very cold. Julian turned up the stove a little more, to heat the room better.

George cuddled Timmy and was soon as warm as toast, but the others lay awake, trying to get their cold hands and feet warm again. Julian felt very puzzled. So there *was* a lot of truth in that woman's peculiar tale, after all!

They awoke late the next morning, for they had been tired out with their exertions the day before, and with the excitements in the night. Julian leapt out of his bunk when he found that it was actually ten to nine, and dressed quickly, calling to the others. He went out to get some snow to put into the kettle.

Soon breakfast was ready, for Anne was next to get up, and she began quickly to prepare some food. Boiled eggs and ham, bread, butter and jam – and good hot cocoa again. Soon they were all eating and chattering, talking over the happenings of the night, which somehow didn't seem nearly so remarkable now that daylight was everywhere, brilliant with snow, and the sun trying to come from behind the clouds.

As they sat round the table, eating and talking, Timmy ran to the door and began to bark. 'Now what's up?' said Dick. Then a face looked in at the window!

It was a remarkable face, old, lined and wrinkled yet curiously young-looking too. The eyes were as blue as a summer day. It was a man's face, with a long, raggedy beard and a moustache.

'Gracious – he looks like one of the old prophets out of the Bible,' said Anne, really startled. 'Who is he?'

'The shepherd, I expect,' said Julian, going to the door. 'We'll ask him in for a cup of cocoa. Maybe he can answer a few questions for us!'

He opened the door. 'Are you the shepherd?' he said. 'Come in. We're having breakfast and we can give you some too, if you like.'

The shepherd came in, and smiled, making many more wrinkles appear on his weather-beaten face.

Julian wondered if he spoke English, or only Welsh. He was a fine-looking fellow, tall and straight, and obviously much younger than he looked.

'You are kind,' he said, standing there with his crook, and Anne suddenly felt that there must have been men just like this all through the history of the world, ever since there had been sheep on the hills, and men to watch them.

The shepherd spoke slowly, as English words were not easy for him. 'You want to send – to send – words – to the farm?' he said, in the lilting Welsh voice so pleasant to hear.

'Oh yes – please take a message to the farm,' said Julian, handing him some bread and butter, and a dish of cheese. 'Just say we're fine, and all is well.'

'All is well, all is well,' repeated the shepherd, and refused the bread and cheese. 'No. I won't eat now. But I would like a drink, please, for the morning is cold.'

'Shepherd,' said Julian, 'did you hear curious noises last night – rumblings and grumblings – and did you feel shudderings and see a coloured mist over the hill there?'

The shepherd listened intently, trying to follow the strange English words. He understood that Julian was asking him something about the opposite hill. He took a sip of his cocoa, and looked over to the hill. 'It has always been a strange hill,' he said slowly, pronouncing some of his words oddly, so that they were hard to understand. 'My grandad told me a big dog lay below, growling for food, and my nan said witches lived there and made their spells, and – and the smock rose up . . .'

'Smock? What does he mean by that?' said George.

'He means "smoke" I should think,' said Julian.

'Don't interrupt. Let him talk. This is very interesting.'

'The smock rose up, and we saw it in the sky,' went
on the shepherd, his forehead wrinkled with the effort
of using words he was not familiar with. 'And it comes
still, young ones, it comes still! The big dog growls,
the witches cook in their pots, and the smock rises.'

'We heard the big dog growling last night, and saw
the witches' smoke,' said Anne, quite under the spell
of the lilting voice of the old shepherd.

The man looked at her and smiled. 'Yes,' he said.
'Yes. But the dog is worse now and the witches are
more evil – more wicked, much more wicked . . .'

'More wicked?' said Julian. 'How?'

The shepherd shook his head. 'I am not clever,' he
said. 'I know few things – my sheep, and the wind and
the sky – and I know too that the hill is wicked – yes,
more wicked. You must not go near it, young ones! For
there the plough will not plough the fields, the spade
will not dig, and neither will the fork.'

This somehow sounded so much like a piece out of
the Old Testament that the children felt quite solemn.
What a strange and impressive old man!

'He thinks long, long thoughts all the hours he sits
watching his sheep,' thought Julian, gazing at him.
'No wonder he says extraordinary things. But what
does he mean about the plough not ploughing the
fields, I wonder?'

The shepherd put his cup down on the table. 'I go
now,' he said. 'and I take your words to Mrs Jones.
And thank you for your kindess. Good day!'

He went out with great dignity, and the children
saw him striding past the window, his beard being
blown backwards by the wind.

'Well!' said Dick. 'What a character! I almost felt

that I was in church, listening to a preacher. I liked him, didn't you? But what did he mean about ploughs not ploughing and spades not digging? That's nonsense!'

'Well – it may not be,' said Julian, 'After all, we know that our car wouldn't go down that hill fast – and you remember that Aily's mother – the shepherd's wife – said that the postman had to leave his bicycle at the bottom of the hill – even that wouldn't work! So it's quite likely that in the old days ploughs went too heavily and too slowly to plough properly, and that spades were the same.'

'But why?' said Anne, puzzled. 'Surely you don't *really* believe these things? I know our own car went crawling down – but that *might* have been because something went wrong in its works for a little while!'

'Anne doesn't *want* to believe in ploughs and spades and forks that won't do their jobs!' said Dick, teasingly. 'Come on – let's forget the weird happenings last night and put on our skis. I feel pretty stiff after yesterday – but a bit of skiing down those slopes will do me good. What about it?'

'Yes! Come on!' said Julian. 'Buck up with the clearing away, and we can get out the skis. Hurry!'

12 Out on the hills

Timmy didn't find skiing any fun at all, because, not being fitted with skis, he couldn't keep up with the others, when they tore down the hill at top speed!

At first he plunged after them, but when he jumped into a great soft heap of snow, and buried himself completely, he decided that this kind of winter sport was not for him! He clambered out of the snow-heap, shook the snow off his coat, and stared forlornly after the shouting children.

They had skied before, and were quite good at it. The hill down which they went was very long, and had a fine slope. It ran smoothly into the upward slope of the next hill, on which Old Towers House had been built.

Julian did a marvellous run down, and went swinging on up the opposite hill. He called to the others.

'I say – what about going up to the top of *this* hill, because we're already part of the way up – and skiing down, and partly up our own slope again. It would save time, and give us a jolly good second ski-run.'

All but Anne thought this was a very good idea. She said nothing, and Dick looked at her.

'She's scared of going up Old Towers Hill!' he said. 'Are you afraid of the big, big dog, Anne, who lies under it and growls at night, or of the lank-haired witches that sit on the hill and make their smoky spells?'

'Don't be silly,' said Anne, cross with Dick for reading her thoughts. She didn't believe in either dogs or witches, but somehow she did *not* like that hill! 'I'm coming too, of course!'

So she toiled up the opposite hill with the others, quite ready to enjoy the lovely run down, and to end halfway up their own hill.

'Look – you can see Old Towers quite clearly now,' said George to Julian. She was right. There, not far off, was the great old house, set with towers, built cosily into the side of the steep hill.

They stood still and looked at it. 'We can even see down into a few of the rooms,' said Julian. 'I wonder if the old lady is still there – Mrs Thomas – the one that Aily's mother used to go and work for?'

'Poor old thing – I'm sorry for her if she is,' said George. 'Seeing nobody – keeping out all her friends! I wish we could go and inquire at the house for something – pretend we've lost our way, and snoop round a bit. But there's that fierce dog.'

'Yes – we don't want any more fights,' said Julian. 'Now – we're almost at the top. We'll wait for the others and then have a race. What a wonderful slope!'

'Julian, look – is that someone at one of the tower windows – the one to the right?' said George suddenly, as they stood waiting, looking down at the big old house some way off below them. Julian looked at the tower at once, just in time to see someone disappear.

'Yes. It *was* someone!' he said. 'Someone staring at us, I think. I expect no one ever comes near this hill, and it must have been a surprise to look out and see *us*! Did you make out if it was a man or a woman?'

'A woman, I *think*,' said George. 'Could it have been old Mrs Thomas, do you think? Oh, Ju – you don't suppose she's being kept prisoner in that tower, do you – while her horrid son and his friends gradually steal everything? You know we heard that vans went up to the house in the middle of the night.'

'Hallo, you two!' said Dick, labouring up with Anne. 'What a climb! Still, the run down will be worth it. I simply *must* have a rest first, though!'

'Dick, George and I thought we saw someone at the tower window there – the one on the right,' said Julian. 'When we get back we'll get our field-glasses and train them on to that window. We might *possibly* see some sign of someone there!'

Dick and Anne stared hard at the tower window – and as they looked, someone drew the curtains swiftly across!

'There – we've been seen – and we're not going to be encouraged to look at the old place!' said Julian. 'No wonder there are strange stories about it! Come on, now – let's start our run down!'

They set off together, each taking a different line. Whooooooosh! The wind blew in their faces as they flew down the white slope, gasping in delight at their speed. Julian and Anne slid swiftly all the way down the first slope and halfway up the next – but Dick and George were not so fortunate. They both caught their skis in something, and shot into the air and then down into the soft snow. They lay there breathless, almost dazed with the sudden stoppage.

'Whew!' said Dick, at last. 'What a shock! Is that you, George? Are you all right?'

'I think so,' said George. 'One ankle feels a bit funny – no, I think it's all right! Hallo, here's Tim! He must have seen us fall, and come rushing down to help. It's all right, Tim. We're not hurt. It's all part of the fun!'

As they lay there, getting their breath, halfway

down the first slope, a loud voice shouted in the distance.

'Hey there! You keep off this slope!'

Dick sat up straight at once. He saw a tall fellow wading through the snow towards them, coming from the direction of Old Towers, looking angry.

'We're only skiing!' shouted back Dick. 'And we're not doing any harm! Who are you?'

'I'm the caretaker,' shouted the man, nodding his head towards Old Towers. 'This field belongs to the house. So keep off it!'

'We'll come and ask permission of the owners,' yelled Dick, standing up, thinking this might be a good way of having a look at the house.

'You can't. There's no one else here but me!' shouted back the man. 'I'm the caretaker, I tell you. I'll set my dog on you all, if you don't do what I say!'

'That's funny,' said Dick to George, as the man waded back through the snow. 'He says he's the only one in the house – and yet we saw someone in the right-hand tower only a few minutes ago! The care-taker wouldn't have had time to have got here from the tower – so he *isn't* the only one in the house. There is someone in the tower as well. Odd, isn't it?'

George had held Timmy by the collar all the time the man was speaking. Timmy had growled at the man's angry voice, and George was afraid he might fly at him. Then, if the other dog appeared, there might be a fight! That would be dreadful! Timmy might get bitten again.

She and Dick tried their skis to see if they were still properly fixed after their fall – and then went gliding smoothly off again. The others were waiting for them at the top of the hill.

'Who was that man? What was he shouting about?'

demanded Julian. 'Did he actually come from Old Towers?'

'Yes – and a surly fellow he was, too,' said Dick. 'He ordered us to keep off that slope – said it belonged to Old Towers and he was the caretaker – and when we said we'd go and ask permission from the owners, he said he was the only one in the house! But *we* know different.'

'Yes. We do,' said Julian, puzzled. 'Why should it matter to anyone if we ski down that particular slope? Are they afraid we might see something in the house – as we did! And why tell a lie and say there was no one else there? Did he *sound* like a caretaker?'

'Well – he didn't sound *Welsh*!' said George, 'And I should have thought that any owners would have chosen someone trustworthy from the village, someone Welsh, wouldn't you? This is all rather mysterious!'

'And if you add to it all the strange noises and things, it's extremely *curious*,' said Dick. 'In fact, I feel it might be worth inquiring into!'

'No,' said Anne. 'Don't let's spoil our holiday. It's such a short one.'

'Well – I don't see how we *can* inquire into the matter,' said George. 'I'm certainly not going to that house while the dog is there – and there's no other way of making inquiries – even if they would get us anywhere, which I'm pretty sure they wouldn't!'

'I say – do you know that it's almost one o'clock?' said Anne, pleased to change the subject. 'Isn't *any*body hungry?'

'Yes – I'm *ravenous*!' said Julian. 'But as I thought it was only about half-past eleven, I didn't like to mention it! Let's go in and have dinner. I vote we finish up that ham!'

They went to the hut, and there, standing in the snow outside it, were two quart bottles of milk, and a large parcel which Timmy at once went to, wagging his tail eagerly. He gave a little bark.

'He says it's meat, so it must be for him,' said George with a laugh.

Julian tore off the paper and laughed too. 'Well, Timmy's right,' he said. 'It's a big piece of cold roast pork. No ham for me then. I'll have some of this!'

'Pity we haven't any apple sauce,' said Dick. 'I love it with pork.'

'Well, if you like to wait while I make some on the stove, with a few of the apples we brought . . .' began Anne. But the others refused at once. No one was going to wait one minute longer for their meal than they could help, apple sauce or not!

It was a merry meal, and certainly the pork was good. Timmy had a piece and thought that George was very mean not to give him the rest of the joint when they had finished with it.

'Oh no, Tim!' said George, as he put an inquiring paw on her knee. 'Certainly not. *We're* going to finish it up tomorrow! You shall have the bone then.'

'There's more snow coming,' said Julian, looking out of the window. 'I say – who brought the meat and the milk here, do you think?'

'The shepherd, I should imagine, on his way back,' said Dick. 'Jolly nice of him. I wonder where that kid Aily is? I'd be scared of her getting caught in the snow, and having to sleep on the hills in it.'

'I expect she'll look after herself all right *and* her lamb and dog!' said Julian. 'I'd like to see her again – but unless she's hungry, I don't expect we shall!'

'Talk of an angel and hear the rustle of her wings!' said Anne. 'Here she is!' And sure enough, there was

Aily, looking in at the window, holding up her lamb for him to take a peep too!

'Let's get her in and feed her – and ask her if *she* knows who lives in Old Towers,' said George. 'She might have seen someone in that right-hand tower too, as we did!'

'Right. I'll call her in,' said Julian, going to the door. 'She *might* know something – always scouring round about the countryside!'

He was right! Aily *did* know something – something that interested everyone very much!

13 Aily is surprising

Aily was not shy this time. She did not run away when Julian opened the door. She was still dressed in the same few clothes, but her face glowed, and she certainly didn't *look* cold!

'Hallo, Aily!' said Julian. 'Come along in. We're having dinner – and there is plenty for you!'

Her dog ran right up to the door and into the room, when he smelt the dinner there. Timmy looked most surprised, and gave a very small growl.

'No, Tim, no – he's your guest,' said George. 'Remember your manners, please!'

The small dog wagged his tail vigorously. 'There, Timmy! He's telling you not to be afraid of him; *he* won't hurt you!' said Anne, which made everyone laugh. Timmy wagged his tail vigorously, too, and the pair were friends at once.

Aily came in then, the lamb in her arms, in case Timmy might object to him. But Timmy didn't. He was very interested in the little creature, and when Aily set him down and let him run about the room, Timmy ran sniffing after him, his tail still wagging fast.

Anne offered the untidy little girl some of the meat but she shook her head and pointed at the cheese. 'Aily like,' she said, and looked on in delight as Anne cut her a generous piece. She sat down on the floor to eat it, and the lamb came along and nibbled at it too. It really was a dear little thing.

'Fany bach!' said the child, and kissed his little nose.

'"Bach" is Welsh for "little", isn't it?' said Anne. She touched Aily on the arm. 'Aily bach!' she said, and the child smiled a sudden sweet smile at her.

'Where did you sleep last night, Aily?' asked George. 'Your mother was looking for you.'

But she had spoken too quickly, and Aily didn't understand. George repeated her words slowly.

Aily nodded. 'In the hay,' she said. 'Down at Magga Farm.'

'Aily, listen – who lives at Old Towers?' said Julian, speaking as slowly and clearly as he could.

'Many people,' said Aily, pointing to the cheese, to show that she wanted another piece. 'Big men, little men. Big dog, too. More big than him!' and she pointed at Timmy.

The others looked at one another in surprise. Many men! Whatever were they doing at Old Towers?

'And yet the caretaker fellow said he was the only one there!' said George.

'Aily, listen – is there – an – old – lady – there?' asked Julian, slowly. 'An – old – lady?'

Aily nodded her head. 'Yes – one old lady – I see her high up in tower – sometimes she does not see Aily. Aily hide.'

'Where do you hide?' asked Dick, curiously.

'Aily won't tell, will never tell,' said the child, looking through half-closed eyes at Dick, as if she kept her secrets behind them.

'Did you see the old lady when you were in the fields?' asked Julian. Aily considered this, and shook her head.

'Well, where then?' asked Julian. 'Look – you shall

have some of this chocolate if you can tell me.' He held
the bar of chocolate just out of her reach. She looked at
it with bright eyes. Obviously chocolate was a rare
treat for her. She reached out suddenly for it, but Julian
was too quick for her.

'No. You tell me what I ask you,' he said. '*Then* you
shall have the chocolate.'

Aily suddenly hit out with her hands and gave him a
good punch in the chest. He laughed and took both her
small hands in his big one.

'No, Aily, no. I am your friend. You do not hit a
friend.'

'*I* know where you were, when you saw the old
lady!' said Dick, slyly. 'Aily – you were in the grounds
– in the garden!'

'How do you know?' cried Aily. She dragged her
hands out of Julian's hand, and leapt to her feet, facing
Dick, looking furious and frightened.

'Here – don't get so upset,' said Dick, astonished.

'How do you know?' demanded Aily again. 'You
haven't told anyone?'

'Of course I've told no one,' said Dick, who had
only just thought of the idea that very moment. 'Aha!
So you get into the grounds of Old Towers, do you?
How do you get in?'

'Aily won't tell,' said the little girl, and suddenly
burst into tears. Anne put her arm round her to
comfort her, but the child pushed it roughly away. 'He
– Dai went there, not me, not Aily. Poor Dai – big dog
bark, wuff-wuff, like that – and . . . and . . .'

'And so you went in to get Dai, didn't you?' said
Dick. 'Good little Aily, brave Aily.'

The little girl rubbed her tears away with a grubby
hand, and left black streaks down her cheeks. She
smiled at Dick, and nodded. 'Good Aily!' she re-

peated, and took the little dog on her knee and hugged him. 'Poor Dai bach!'

'So she got into the grounds, did she?' said Julian, in a low voice to Dick. 'I wonder how? Through the hedge perhaps. Aily – we want to see this old lady. Can we get through the hedge round the garden?'

'No,' said Aily, shaking her head vigorously. 'There's a fence – a big high fence that bites.'

Everyone laughed at the idea of a biting fence. But George guessed what she meant. 'An electric fence!' she said. 'So that's what they've put round. My word – the place is like a fort! Locked gates, a fierce dog, an electric fence!'

'How on earth did Aily get in, then?' said Dick. 'Aily – have you seen this old woman many times? Has she seen *you*?'

Aily didn't understand and he had to ask his question again, more simply. The child nodded her head.

'Aily see her many times – up high – and one time she see Aily. She throw out papers – little bits – out of the window.'

'Aily – did you pick them up?' said Julian, sitting up straight at once. 'Was there writing on them?' Everyone waited for Aily's answers. She nodded her head.

'Yes. Writings like they do at school – pen writings.'

'Did you read any of them?' asked Dick.

Aily suddenly wore a hunted expression. She shook her head – then she nodded it. 'Yes, Aily read them,' she said. 'They say "Good morning, Aily. How are you, Aily?"'

'Does the old woman *know* you then?' asked Dick, surprised.

'No, she doesn't know Aily – only Aily's mam,' said the child. 'She wrote on her papers "Aily, you good girl. Aily, you very good!"'

'She's not telling the truth now,' said Dick, noticing that the child would not look at them when she spoke. 'I wonder why?'

'I think *I* know,' said Anne. She took a piece of paper and wrote on it clearly. 'Good morning, Aily.' Then she showed it to the child. 'Read that, Aily,' she said.

But Aily couldn't! She had no idea what was written on the paper.

'She can't even *read*,' said Anne. 'And she was ashamed, so she pretended she could. Never mind, Aily! Listen – have you any of those bits of paper that the old woman dropped?'

Aily felt about in her few clothes, and at last produced a piece of paper that looked as if it had been torn from the top of a page in a book. She gave it to Dick.

All the four bent over it, reading what was written there, in small, rather illegible writing.

'I want help. I am a prisoner here, in my own house, while terrible things go on. They have killed my son. Help me, help me! Bronwen Thomas.'

'Good gracious!' said Julian, very startled. 'I say – this is extraordinary, isn't it! Do you think we ought to show it to the police?'

'Well – there is probably only one policeman shared between three or four of these little places,' said Dick. 'And there's another thing – the old lady *might* be off her head, you know. What she says may not be true.'

'How can we possibly find out if it is or not?' said George.

Dick turned to Aily. 'Aily – we want to see the old lady – we want to take her something nice to eat – she is all by herself, she is sad. Will you show us the way into the grounds?'

'No,' said Aily, shaking her head vigorously. 'Big

dog there – dog with teeth like this!' And she bared her own small white teeth and snarled, much to Timmy's astonishment. The children laughed.

'Well – we can't *make* her tell us,' said Julian. 'And anyway, even if we got into the grounds, that dog would be there – and I don't fancy him, somehow.'

'Aily show you way into house,' suddenly said the small girl, much to everyone's astonishment. They all stared at her.

'Into the *house*!' said Dick. 'But – you'd have to show us the way into the *grounds* first if we are to get into the house, Aily!'

'No,' said Aily, shaking her head. 'Aily show you way to house. Aily do that. No big dog there!'

Just then Timmy began to bark, and someone came by the door, looking in as she passed. It was Aily's mother, who had again been to take some things to her shepherd husband. She saw Aily sitting on the floor and gave an angry shout. Then standing at the door she poured out a long string of Welsh words which the children didn't understand. In a great fright Aily ran straight to a cupboard, her dog and lamb with her.

But it was no good. Her mother stormed into the hut and dragged Aily out, shaking her well. Timmy growled, but Aily's little dog was as frightened as she was, and the lamb bleated pitifully in the child's arms.

'I'm taking Aily home!' said her angry mother, glaring at the four children as if she thought they were responsible for the child's keeping away from home. 'I'll scold her well!'

And out she went, holding the protesting child firmly by one arm. The children could do nothing. After all, she was Aily's mother, and the child really was a little monkey, the way she wandered round the countryside.

'You know – I think we'd better go down to the farm and tell *Morgan* what we know,' said Julian, making up his mind. 'I really do. If this thing is serious – and if the old lady is really a prisoner – I don't see how *we* can do a thing – but Morgan might be able to. He'd know the police for one thing. Come on – let's go down now. We can stay at the farm for the night if it gets dark. Buck up – let's go straightaway!'

14   Morgan is surprising too

George did not particularly want to go down to the farm, as she was afraid of Timmy meeting the farm dogs again, and being attacked. Julian saw her doubtful face and understood.

'Would you like to stay here by yourself with Timmy, George, till we come back?' he said. 'You should be all right with Tim – he'll look after you. The only thing is, will you be scared if any more tremblings and shudderings and shimmerings come again tonight?'

'I'll stay with George,' said Anne. 'It would really be best if you two boys went alone. I'm a bit tired and I don't think I could go as fast as you'd want to.'

'Right. Then Dick and I will go together, and leave you two girls here with Timmy,' said Julian. 'Come on, Dick. If we hurry, we *might* get back before dark.'

They set off together, and went swiftly down the winding mountain path, still white with snow. They were glad when at last they saw the farmhouse. A light was already in the kitchen, and looked very welcoming!

They went in at the front door, and made their way to the big kitchen, where Mrs Jones was washing up at the sink. She turned in astonishment when they came in, stamping the snow from their shoes.

'Well now – this is a surprise!' she said, drying her

hands on a towel. 'Is there something wrong? Where are the girls?'

'They're up at the hut – they're fine,' said Julian.

'You have come for something more to eat?' said Mrs Jones, feeling certain this was the reason for their sudden visit.

'No, thank you – we've got plenty!' said Julian. 'We just wondered if we could talk to your son – Morgan. We – well, we've got something to tell him. Something rather urgent.'

'Well now – what could that be?' said Mrs Jones, all curiosity at once. 'Let me see – yes, Morgan will be up at the big barn.' She pointed out of the window, where a big and picturesque old barn stood, outlined against the evening sky. 'It is there you will find my Morgan. Will you be staying the night, now? You'll like supper – a good supper?'

'Well – yes, we should,' said Julian, suddenly realising that they had missed out tea altogether. 'Thanks awfully. We'll just go and find Morgan.'

They made their way out to the big old barn. Morgan's three dogs at once ran out when they heard strange footsteps, and growled. But they recognised the boys immediately and leapt round them, barking.

The giantlike Morgan came out to see what the dogs were barking about. He was surprised to find the two boys there, fondling the dogs.

'Hey?' he said, questioningly. 'Anything wrong?'

'We think there is,' said Julian. 'May we tell you about it?'

Morgan took them into the almost dark barn. He had been raking it over and he went on with his raking as Julian began his tale.

'It's about Old Towers,' said Julian, and Morgan stopped his raking at once. But he went on again almost immediately, listening without a word.

Julian told him his story. He told him about the rumbling noises, the shimmering in the sky that Dick had seen, the 'shuddering' they had all felt – then about the old woman they had seen in the tower – and how Aily had told of the pieces of paper, and shown them one, wich proved that old Mrs Thomas was a prisoner in her own house.

For the first time Morgan spoke. 'And where is this paper?' he asked in his deep bass voice.

Julian produced it and handed it over. Morgan lit a lamp to look at it, for it was now practically dark.

He read it and put it into his pocket. 'I'd rather like it back,' said Julian, surprised. 'Unless you want it to show the police. What do you think about it all? And is there anything we can do? I don't like to think of . . .'

'I will tell you what you are to do,' said Morgan. 'You are to leave it to *me*, Morgan Jones. You are children, you know nothing. This matter is not for children. I can tell you that. You must go back to the hut, and you must forget all you have heard and all you have seen. And if Aily comes again you must bring her down here to me, and I will talk to her.'

His voice was so hard and determined that the two boys were startled and shocked.

'But, Morgan!' said Julian. 'Aren't you going to do anything about this . . . go to the police, or . . .'

'I have told you this is not a matter for children,' said Morgan. 'I will say no more. You will go back to the hut, and you will say nothing to anyone. If you are not willing to do this, you will go home tomorrow.'

With that the giant of a man put his rake over his shoulder, and left the two boys alone in the barn. 'What do you make of *that*?' said Julian, very angry. 'Come on – we'll go back to the hut. I'm not going to the farm for supper. I don't feel as though I want to meet that rude, dour Morgan again this evening!'

Feeling angry and disappointed the boys made their way out of the barn, towards the path that led up to the hill. It was almost dark now, and Julian felt in his pocket for his torch.

'Blow! I didn't bring it with me!' he said. 'Have you one, Dick?'

Dick hadn't one either, and as neither of them felt like making their way up the mountainside in the darkness Julian decided to go back to the farm, slip up to his bedroom there, and find the extra torch he had put in one of the drawers.

'Come along,' he said to Dick. 'We'll try and get in and out without seeing Morgan or old Mrs Jones.'

They went quietly back to the farmhouse, keeping a look-out for Morgan. Julian slipped up the stone stairway to the bedroom he had been given a few nights before, and rummaged in the drawer for his torch. Good – there it was!

He went downstairs again – and bumped into old Mrs Jones at the bottom. She gave a little scream.

'Oh, it's you, Julian bach! Now what have you been telling my Morgan to put him into such a temper! Enough to turn the milk sour his face is! Wait now, while I get you some supper. Would you like some pork and . . .'

'Well – we've decided to go back to the hut, after all,' said Julian, hoping that the kind old woman wouldn't be upset. 'The girls are alone, you know – and it's dark now.'

'Oh yes, yes – then you shall go back!' said Mrs Jones. 'Wait for one minute – you shall have some of my new bread, and some more pie. Wait now.'

The boys stood in the doorway, waiting, hoping

that Morgan would not come by. They suddenly heard him in the distance, yelling at a dog, in his loud, really fierce voice.

'Taking it out on the dogs, I suppose,' said Julian to Dick. 'Gosh – I wouldn't like to come up against him, if I was one of his men! Strong giant that he is, he could take on a dozen men if he wanted to – or a score of dogs!'

Mrs Jones came up with a net bag full of food. 'Here you are,' she said. 'Take care of those girls – and don't go near Morgan now. He's in a fine temper, is my Morgan, and he is not nice to hear!'

The two boys thoroughly agreed. Morgan was *not* nice to hear. They were glad when they were away up the path, out of reach of his enormous voice!

'Well, that's that,' said Julian. 'No help to be got from *this* quarter! And we're forbidden to do anything at all about the matter. As if we were kids!'

'He kept telling us we were only children,' said Dick, sounding disgusted. 'I can't make it out. Ju, WHY was he so annoyed about it all? Didn't he believe us?'

'Oh yes – he believed us all right,' said Julian. 'If you ask me, I think he knows much more than *we* were able to tell him. There's some kind of racket going on at Old Towers – something peculiar and underhand – and Morgan is in it! That's why he shut us up and told us not to interfere, and to forget all about it! He's in whatever's going on, I'm sure of it.'

Dick whistled. 'My word! So that's why he was so angry. He thought we might be putting a spoke in his wheel. And of course the last thing he would want us to do would be to go to the police! Well – whatever do we do next, Ju?'

'I don't know. We'll have to talk it over with the

girls,' said Julian, worried. 'This *would* crop up just when we're all set for a jolly holiday!'

'Julian, what do you *think* is going on at Old Towers?' asked Dick, puzzled. 'I mean – it isn't only a question of locking up an old lady in a tower – and selling off her goods and taking the money. It's all the other things too – the rumblings and shudderings and that strange mist.'

'Well – apparently *those* things have been going on for some time,' said Julian. 'They may have nothing whatever to do with what Morgan is mixed up in which is, I'm sure, to do with robbing the old lady. In fact, those old tales may be a very good way of keeping people away from the place. In these country places people are much more afraid of strange happenings than townspeople are.'

'It all sounds very convincing when you put it like that,' said Dick. 'But somehow I don't *feel* convinced. I just can't help feeling there's something *strange* about it all – something we don't know!'

They fell silent after that, walking one behind the other on the mountain path, seeing the big black stones looming up one after the other in the light of Julian's torch. It seemed a long, long way in the dark, much longer than in the daylight.

But at last they saw the light in the window of the hut. Thank goodness! They were both very hungry now, and were glad that Mrs Jones had presented them with more food. They could really tuck in.

Timmy barked as soon as they came near, and George let him out of the door. She knew by his bark that it was the boys coming back.

'Oh, we *are* glad you came back, instead of staying down at the farm!' cried Anne. 'What happened? Is Morgan going to the police?'

'No,' said Julian. 'He was angry. He told us not to interfere. He took that bit of paper with the message on, and never gave it back to us. *We* think he's mixed up with whatever is going on!'

'Very well then,' said George at once. '*We'll* take up the matter ourselves! *We'll* find out what's going on and *MOST CERTAINLY we'll* get poor old Mrs Thomas out of that tower. I don't know how – but we'll do it! Won't we, Timmy?'

15 'What's up, Tim?'

The four children sat and talked for a long time, sitting round the little oil-stove, eating a good supper. What would be the best thing to do? It was all very well for George to flare up and say *they* would see to things, *they* would rescue the old lady from the tower – but how could they even *begin* to do anything? For one thing they didn't know how to get into the house! No one was going to risk a battle with that fierce dog!

'If only that kid Aily would help us!' said Julian, at last. 'She's really our only hope. It's no good going to the police – it would take us ages to go down to the village at the bottom of the mountain, and find out where the nearest police station is – and we'd *never* get a village policeman to believe our tale!'

'I wonder the villagers don't do something about Old Towers,' said Dick, puzzled. 'I mean – all those peculiar vibrations we felt last night – and the noises we heard – and the light in the sky when that mist hung over the place . . .'

'Yes – but I suppose all those things are seen and heard up here in the mountains much more clearly than down in the valley below,' said Anne, sensibly. 'I don't expect that weird shuddering would be felt in the valley nor would the rumblings be heard, and even the strange mist over Old Towers might not be seen.'

'That's true,' said Julian. 'I never thought of that. Yes – we up here would see a lot . . . and possibly the shepherd higher up on the hills would, as well. I dare say the farm down below us would see something, too . . . Well, we *know* they did, because of Morgan's behaviour to us tonight! He obviously knew what we were talking about!'

'He's also obviously hand in glove with the men in that place – the big men and little men that Aily spoke of. Gosh – I *wish* she'd show us how to get into that house. How does she get in? I'm blowed if I can think of any way. With that electric fence all round, it sounds impossible.'

'The fence that *bites*!' said George, with a laugh. 'Fancy that child touching the fence and getting a shock. She's an extraordinary creature, isn't she – quite wild!'

'I hope she didn't get told off,' said Anne. 'She *is* a naughty little truant, of course – but you can't help liking her. Does anybody want more cheese? And there are still some apples left – or I could open a tin of pears.'

'I vote for the pears,' said Dick. 'I feel like something really sweet. I say – this stay up here is turning out rather exciting, isn't it?'

'We always seem to run into trouble,' said Anne, going to the cupboard to fetch the tin of pears.

'Give it a better name, Anne, old thing,' said Dick. 'Adventure! *That's* what we're always running into. Some people do, you know – they just can't help it. And we're those sort of people. Jolly good thing too – it makes life exciting!'

Timmy suddenly began to bark, and everyone started up at once. *Now* what was up?

'Let Timmy out,' said Dick. 'With all these funny goings-on I feel as if it would be just as well to let Tim examine anyone coming by here at night!'

Five Get Into a Fix

'Right,' said George, and went to the door – but as she was about to open it, she heard a dog barking outside, just beyond the hut. She swung round.

'I'm not letting Timmy out! That might be Morgan with his dogs! I seem to recognise that deep bark!'

'Someone's coming by,' said Anne, half scared. 'My word – it *is* Morgan!'

So it was. He passed by the window, and they saw his great shoulders and head bent against the wind as he went on up the hill. He didn't even glance in at them – but the three dogs, who were with him, began to bark furiously as they sensed another dog in the hut. Timmy barked back furiously too.

Then all was quiet. Morgan had gone by and the dogs with him. 'Whew – I'm glad you didn't let Tim out as I suggested,' said Dick. 'He'd have been torn to pieces!'

'Where do you suppose Morgan's going?' she asked Anne. It's funny he should be going *up* the hill – not even in the direction of Old Towers!'

'Probably going to talk to the shepherd,' said Julian. 'He's farther up the hill with his sheep. I say – I wonder if *he's* in this too!'

'Oh *no*,' said Anne. 'He's good – I could feel it in my bones. I can't *imagine* him mixed up with a gang of any sort.'

Nobody could, of course. They had all liked the shepherd. But why else would Morgan be going up to him at this time of night?

'He might be going to tell him that we know too much,' suggested Julian. 'He might ask him to keep an eye on us.'

'Or he might be going to complain of Aily, and her doings inside the grounds of Old Towers,' said Dick. 'Goodness – do you suppose that kid will get into

trouble because we told Morgan about her – and gave
him the bit of paper she found?'

They all stared at one another in dismay. Anne
nodded soberly. 'Yes – that's it, of course. Aily will
certainly get into trouble over this – oh, *why* did we
think of telling Morgan what we knew? Poor little
Aily!'

They all felt uncomfortable about Aily. They liked
the wild, other worldly little creature with her pet
lamb and little dog. Now what would happen to her
thanks to them?

None of them felt like playing cards just then. They
sat and talked, wondering if they would hear Morgan
coming back. They knew Timmy would bark if he
did.

Sure enough he began to bark about half-past eight,
and made them all jump. 'That will be Morgan coming back,' said Julian, and they watched the window to
see if his head and shoulders would pass by again. But
they didn't. Neither did any dog bark outside.

Then George saw that Timmy was sitting with his
ears pricked up, and his head on one side. Why? And if
he could really hear something, why didn't he bark
again? She was puzzled.

'Look at Tim,' she said. 'He's heard *something* – and
yet he's not barking. And he doesn't look very
worried either. What's up, Tim?'

Timmy took no notice. He sat there listening intently,
still with his head on one side. What *could* he hear? It was
most tantalising to the others, because not one of them
could hear anything at all. The countryside seemed to
be absolutely quiet at that moment.

Then suddenly Tim jumped up and barked joyfully!
He ran to the door and whined, scraping at the bottom
of it with his paw. He looked back at George and

barked again, as if to say 'Buck up! Open the door!'

'Well!' said Dick, in surprise. 'What's up, Timmy? Has your best friend come to call? Shall we open the door, Julian?'

'I'll go,' said Julian, and went to open the door cautiously. Timmy leapt out at once, barking and whining.

'There's nobody here,' said Julian, astonished. 'Nobody at all! Hey, Tim, what's all the fuss about? Give me that torch, Dick, will you? I'll go out after him and see what the excitement is.'

Out he went, and flashed the torch around to find Timmy. Ah – there he was, scraping at the little wooden bunker that held the oil-cans and the big enamel jug. Julian was astonished.

'Whatever's come over you, Tim?' he said. 'There's nothing here in this bunker – look, I'll lift the lid so that you can peep inside and see, silly dog!'

He lifted up the lid, and shone his torch inside, to show Timmy that it was empty.

But it wasn't! Julian almost let the lid drop down in his surprise! Someone was there – someone small and half-frozen! It was Aily!

'Aily!' said Julian, hardly believing his eyes. 'What on earth – Aily – what *are* you doing here?'

Aily blinked up at him, looking scared to death. She clutched the lamb and the dog, and didn't say a word. Julian saw that she was shivering, and crying bitterly.

'Poor little Aily bach!' he said, using the only Welsh word he knew. 'Come into the hut – we'll get you warm and make you better.'

The child shook her head and clutched her animals closer. But Julian was not going to leave her there in the little oil-bunker on that cold night! He lifted her up, animals and all, and cuddled her. Aily strove to get free but his arms were strong and held her close.

George's voice came impatiently from the hut. 'Ju! Tim! Where are you? Have you found anything?'

'Yes,' called back Julian. 'We have. We're bringing it along – it's quite a surprise!'

He carried the shivering child into the hut, and the others stared in the utmost astonishment. Aily! A cold, forlorn and miserable little Aily, pale and shivering! And the lamb and dog too!

'Bring her near the stove,' said Anne, and stroked the child's thin arm. 'Poor Aily!'

Julian tried to set her down, and the animals as well, but she clung to him. She sensed that he was good and kind and strong, and his arms were very comforting. Julian sat down on a chair, still holding the little creature closely. The dog and lamb slid off his knee and ran sniffing round the room.

'She was in the oil-bunker out there – she and the lamb and dog,' he said. 'All cuddled up together. Partly hiding, I should think, and partly for shelter. Maybe she's slept there before, with these two. Isn't she a poor little mite? She seems very unhappy. Let's give her something to eat.'

'I'll make some hot cocoa,' said Anne. 'George, get some bread and butter and cheese for her – and hadn't we better get the lamb and dog something too? What do you give lambs?'

'Milk out of a bottle,' said Dick. 'But we haven't got a feeding-bottle! I dare say it will lap milk. Good gracious – the things that happen here!'

Aily felt warm and comforted in Julian's arms. She lay there like a little animal, too cold and tired to be scared. Julian was glad to hold her and comfort her. Poor little thing – what had made her come this long way so late at night?

'She must have gone home with her mother,' he said, watching the little dog hobnobbing with a delighted Timmy. 'And probably got a good telling off, and was shut up somewhere. And then my guess is that Morgan went down to see if she was there, and to scold her, and tell her mother to be sure and not let her out, and . . .'

'Morgan!' repeated Aily, sitting up in fear, looking all round as if he might be there. 'Morgan! No! No!'

'It's all right, little thing,' said Julian. 'We'll look after you. Morgan shan't get you!'

'See?' he said to the others. 'I bet I'm right! It was he who went and scared her – as soon as he was gone, I expect she escaped from her mother's house and came up here to hide. That horrible fellow! If he shouted at her as he shouted at us, she'd be scared stiff. I bet he was afraid she'd go and give more of the game away unless she was shut up – might even show us the way into the old house over on the opposite hill!'

Timmy suddenly gave a bark – but not a joyful one this time! Anne cried out at once, 'That may be Morgan coming back! Hide Aily, for goodness sake – or he'll drag her out of here and take her back with him! Quick – where shall we hide her?'

16   *Aily changes her mind*

Aily leapt out of Julian's arms as quickly and surely as a
cat, when she heard that it might be Morgan coming.
She looked round the room like a hunted thing, and
then darted to the bunk beds. With an amazing leap,
she was up on one of the top ones in a trice, and pulled
a rug over her. She lay absolutely still. The lamb
looked up in surprise and bleated.

Then it too leapt up the bunks, as sure-footed as a
goat, and cuddled down with its little mistress. Only
Dai the dog was left below, whining miserably
'Gosh!' said Dick amazed at these incredibly sudden
happenings. 'Look at that! Did you ever see such
leaping! Shut up barking, Tim. We want to hear if
Morgan *is* coming. Ju – where shall we hide Aily's
dog? He mustn't be seen – or heard either!'

Julian lifted the dog up to the top bunk and put him
with the other two there. 'That's about the only place
where he'll keep quiet!' he said. 'Aily – lie quite still till
we tell you everything is safe.'

There was no reply from the bunk – not a word or a
bark or a bleat. Then Timmy began to bark loudly
again, and ran to the door.

'I'm going to *lock* the door,' said Julian. 'I'm not
having Morgan and his dogs in here, hunting for Aily!
My guess is that he knows she's escaped from her
mother's – or maybe she ran off when he scolded her –
and thinks she went to her father, the old shepherd!

He's got to get hold of her, to stop her from spreading what she knows!'

'Well – for goodness sake don't let those dogs in here!' said George, desperately. 'I can hear them barking away in the distance.'

'Quick – let's sit round the table with the cards, and pretend to be playing a game!' said Dick, snatching the cards from a shelf. 'Then if Morgan looks in, he'll think everything is normal – and won't guess we've got Aily here. I bet he'll be sly enough to try and peep in without us seeing him – hoping to spot Aily if we've got her!'

They sat round the table, and Dick dealt out the cards. Anne's hands were trembling, and George felt a bit weak at the knees. Anne kept dropping her cards, and Dick laughed at her.

'Butterfingers! Cheer up – Morgan won't eat you! Now – if I suddenly say "What ho!" you'll know I can see Morgan peeping in at the window, and you must laugh and play like anything. See?'

Dick was the one facing the window, and he kept a sharp eye on it as they played snap. There was no sound of dogs barking now, though Tim sat by the door, his ears cocked, as if he could hear *some*thing.

'Snap!' said Julian, and gathered up the cards. They went on playing.

'Snap!' I say, don't grab like that – you've almost broken my nail!'

'Snap! I said it first!'

'*What ho!*' said Dick, and that put everyone on their guard at once. They went on playing, but without giving much attention to the game now. What could Dick see?

Dick could see quite a lot. He could see a shadowy

face some way from the window, looking in – yes, it was Morgan all right.'

'What ho!' said Dick again, to warn the others that there was still danger. 'WHAT HO!'

Morgan's face had now come quite near to the window. He evidently thought that no one saw him, and that they were all too engrossed in their game to notice anything else. His eyes swept the room from corner to corner. Then his face disappeared.

'He's gone from the window,' said Dick, in a low voice. 'But go on playing. He may come to the door.'

KNOCK! KNOCK!

'Yes – there he is,' said Dick. 'Ju – you take charge now.'

'Who's there?' yelled Julian.

'Morgan. Let me in,' said Morgan's deep, growling voice.

'No – we've got our dog here, and we don't want him set on again,' said Julian, determined not to let Morgan in at any cost.

Morgan turned the handle – but the door was locked. He growled again.

'Sorry! But we can't unlock it!' shouted Julian. 'Our dog might rush out and bite you. He's growling like anything already!'

'Bark, Tim,' said George, in a low voice, and Timmy obligingly barked the place down!

Morgan gave up. 'If you see Aily, send her home,' he said. 'She's gone again, and her mam's worried. I've been looking for her this cold night.'

'Right!' called Julian. 'If she comes we'll give her a bed here.'

'No. You send her home,' shouted. Morgan. 'And pay heed to what I told you down at the barn, or it will be the worse for all of us!'

'For *all* of us! I like *that*!' said Dick, in disgust. 'It will certainly be the worse for him and his friends when the secret's out! Awful fellow! Has he gone, Tim?'

Timmy came away from the door and lay down peacefully. He gave a little bark as if to say 'All clear!'

When the dogs began to bark right away in the distance Tim took no notice. 'That means they're doing down the hill with Morgan, back to the farm,' said George, thankfully. 'We can get Aily down now, and give her something to eat.'

She went to the bunk. 'Aily!' she called, 'Morgan is gone. Gone right away! Come down and have a meal. We will give the lamb some milk and your dog some meat and biscuits!'

Aily's head peered cautiously over the side of the little bunk bed. With a leap she was down on the floor, as lightly as the lamb itself, which followed at once, landing squarely on its four tiny hooves. The little dog had to be lifted out – he was much too scared to jump!

To everyone's amusement, Aily ran straight to Julian, and held up her arms to be taken into his. She felt safe with this big kind boy. He sat down with her on his knees and she cuddled up to him like a kitten.

George put some bread and butter and cheese on the table in front of her, and Anne put down a dish of milk for the lamb, which lapped it greedily but most untidily. The dog tried to get the milk too, but soon went to the dish of cut-up meat and biscuits put down by Anne.

'There – the Aily-family is fed,' she said. 'My word – what an excitement all this is! Julian, don't let Aily gobble like that – she'll be sick. I never did see anyone eat so quickly. She can't have had anything since the bit of cheese we gave her this afternoon!'

Aily snuggled back into Julian's arms contentedly,

when she had eaten every scrap of her meal. She looked up at him, wanting to please him.

'Aily tell how to get into big big house,' she said suddenly, taking everyone completely by surprise. Julian looked down at her. He had the dog on his knee now too, though he would not allow the lamb to climb on as well.

'Aily tell me?' he said gravely. 'Good little Aily bach!'

Aily began to try and tell him. 'Big, big hole,' she began. 'Down, down, down . . .'

'Where's this big hole?' asked Julian.

'High up,' said Aily. 'Down it goes down . . .'

'But where *is* it?' asked Julian again.

Aily went off into a long stream of Welsh and the children listened helplessly. How maddening to have Aily willing to tell them her secret — and then not be able to follow what she said.

'Good little Aily,' said Julian, when she came to a stop at last. 'Where is this big, big hole?'

Aily gazed at him in reproach. 'Aily tell you, tell you, tell you!' she said.

'Yes, I know — but I don't understand Welsh,' said Julian, gently, despairing of trying to make the child understand. 'Where is this big hole — that's all I want to know.'

Aily stared at him. Then she smiled. 'Aily show,' she said, and slipped of his knee. 'Aily show! Come!'

'Good gracious! Not *now*,' said Julian. 'Not in all this snow and darkness. No, Aily — tomorrow — in the morning — not now!'

Aily took a look out of the window into the darkness. She nodded. 'Not now. In the morning, yes? Aily show in the morning.'

'Well, thank goodness that's settled!' said Julian. 'I'd

dearly love to see this big, big hole, whatever it is, now, straightaway – but we'd only get lost on these hills in the dark. We'll look forward to it tomorrow!'

'Good!' said Dick, yawning. 'I must say that I think that's best too. What a bit of luck that Aily's so grateful to you, Ju! I believe she'd do anything in the world for you now.'

'I believe she would too, funny little creature,' said Julian, looking at Aily as she curled up on the rug near the stove, with her lamb and dog beside her. 'How could Morgan scare such a harmless little thing? He's a brute!'

'Jolly good thing he didn't see her when he looked in,' said George. 'He'd probably have broken the door down! One blow of his fist and it would have cracked from top to bottom!'

Everyone laughed. 'Well – good thing it didn't come to that!' said Julian. 'Now then, let's get to bed. We may have *quite* an exciting day tomorrow!'

'I hope we manage to get to that poor old woman in her tower,' said Anne. 'That's the most important thing to do. Aily, you can sleep in that topmost bunk, where you hid. I'll give you some rugs, and a blanket and a pillow.'

It wasn't long before the hut was quiet and peaceful, with all five children in their bunks, and Timmy with George. The lamb and the little dog were with Aily. Julian looked out from his bunk and smiled. What a collection of people and animals in the hut tonight! Well – he was quite glad there were two dogs!

No one woke in the night except George. She felt Timmy stir and sat up, resting on her elbow. But he didn't bark. He gave her a small lick, and sat with her, listening.

The strange rumbling noise was coming again – and

then the 'shuddering', though not so strongly as before. George felt the wooden edge of her bunk – it vibrated as if machinery was in the room below, shaking everything a little.

She leaned out of her bunk and looked out of the window. Her eyes widened as she saw what Dick had seen the other night – the 'shimmering' in the sky. She could think of no other name for that strange quivering that rose and rose and finally ended very high up indeed, seeming to lose itself in the stars that were now shining brightly.

George didn't wake the others. As soon as the weird happenings stopped, she lay down again. Perhaps tomorrow they would know what caused such strange things – yes, tomorrow would be *very* exciting!

17 The 'big, big hole'

Next morning everyone was awake early. They had slept well, and were full of beans – and excited to think that an adventure lay ahead. To get into that old house, with its many secrets, would be marvellous!

Aily followed Julian about the room like a little dog. She wanted to have her breakfast on his knee, just as she had her supper the night before, and he let her. He was ready to do anything she wanted – if only she would show them the way into Old Towers!

'We'd better set off pretty soon,' said Anne, looking out of the window. 'It's snowing pretty fast again – we don't want to get lost!'

'No. That's true. If Aily is going to take us across country, we shan't have the faintest idea where we're going in this heavy snow!' said Julian, rather anxiously.

'I'll just clear up a bit,' then we'll go, shall we?' said Anne. 'Do we take any food with us, Ju?'

'We certainly do – all of us,' said Julian, at once. 'Goodness knows what time we'll get back to this hut. George, you make sandwiches with Anne, will you? And put in some bars of chocolate too, and some apples if there are any left.'

'And for pity's sake, let's remember our torches,' said Dick.

Aily watched while the sandwiches were made, and scraped up the bits that fell on the table to give to

Dai, her small dog. The lamb frisked about, quite at home, getting into everyone's way. But nobody minded it – it was such a charming little long-leggitty creature!

At last all the sandwiches were made and put into two bags. The hut was cleared up and tidied, and the children got into their outdoor clothes.

'I think it would be easiest to toboggan down the slope, and halfway up Old Towers' slope,' said Julian, looking out into the snow. 'It would take us ages to walk – and it's no good skiing, because Aily hasn't any skis – and couldn't use them if she had!'

'Oh yes – let's take the toboggans!' said George, pleased. 'What do we do with the lamb? Leave it here? And must we take Dai the dog, too?'

However, that was not for them to settle! Aily absolutely refused to go without her lamb and dog. She gathered them up into her arms, looking mutinous, when Julian suggested they should be left in the warm hut. Neither would she allow herself to be wrapped up warmly – and only consented to wear a scarf and a woollen hat because they happened to be exactly the same as Julian was wearing!

They set off at last. The snow was still falling, and Julian felt seriously doubtful whether they would be able to find their way down the hill and up the other slope without losing their sense of direction.

The toboggans were rather crowded! Julian and Dick were on the first one, with Aily and the lamb between them, and Anne and George were on the second one, with Timmy and Dai between *them*. George was at the front, and Anne had the awkward job of hanging on to both the dogs and keeping her balance too!

'I know we shall all roll off,' she said to George.

'Good gracious – I half wish we had waited a bit! The snow is falling very fast now!'

'Good thing!' called Julian. 'No one will spot us when we are near Old Towers – they won't be able to see a thing through this snow!'

Julian's toboggan shot off down the snowy slope. It gathered speed, and the boys gasped in delight at the pace. Aily clung to Julian's back, half frightened, and the lamb stared with astonished eyes, not daring to move from its place, squashed in between Aily and Julian!

Whoooooooosh! Down the slope to the bottom, and up the opposite slope, gradually slowing down! Julian's toboggan came to a stop, and then, not far behind, came George's, slowing down too. George got out and dragged her toboggan over to Julian.

'Well,' she said, Her face glowing, 'what do we do now? Wasn't that a wonderful run?'

'Wonderful!' said Julian. 'I only wish we could have a few more! Did you like that, Aily?'

'No,' said Aily, pulling her woollen cap to exactly the same angle that Julian wore his. 'No. It makes my nose cold, so cold.'

She cupped her hand over her nose to make it warm. George laughed.

'Fancy complaining about a cold nose when she's hardly wearing anything on her skinny little body – you'd think the *whole* of her would feel cold – not just her nose!'

'Aily – do you know where the big hole is?' asked Julian, looking about in the snow. The snowflakes were quite big now, and nothing that was more than a few yards away could be seen. Aily stood there, her feet sinking into the snow. She looked all round, and Julian felt certain that she was going to say that she

didn't know which way to go, in this thick snow.
Even he was rather doubtful which was the way back
up the hill!

But Aily was like a dog. She had a sure sense of
direction, and could go from one place to another on a
dark night or in the snow without any difficulty at all!

She nodded.

'Aily know – Dai know, too.'

She walked a few steps, but her feet sank into the
snow about her ankles, and her thin shoes were soon
soaked through.

'She'll get her feet frost-bitten,' said Dick. 'Better
put her on one of the toboggans and pull her, Ju. Pity
we didn't have any snow-boots small enough to lend
her. I say – this is a bit of a crazy expedition, isn't it! I
hope to goodness Aily knows where's she's taking us. I
haven't the foggiest idea at the moment which is east
or west, north or south!'

'Wait – I've got a compass in one of my pockets,'
said Julian, and did a lot of digging in his clothes. At
last he pulled out a small compass. He looked at it.

'That's south,' he said, pointing, 'so that's where
Old Towers Hill is – south is directly opposite our hut;
we know that because the sun shone straight in at our
front windows. I reckon we walk this way, then – due
south.'

'Let's see which way Aily points,' said Dick. He set
her on his tobaggon, and wrapped her scarf more
closely round her. 'Now – which way, Aily?'

Aily at once pointed due south. Everyone was most
impressed.

'That's right,' said Julian. 'Come on, Dick – I'll pull
Aily's toboggan, you can pull the girls' for them.'

They all set off up the rest of the slope of Old
Towers Hill, Aily on the toboggan with Dai and Fany

the lamb, and Timmy sitting in state on George's toboggan, the girls walking behind. Timmy was enjoying himself. He didn't like the way his legs went down into the snow when he tried to run – it was much easier to sit on the toboggan and be pulled along!

'Lazy thing!' said George, and Timmy wagged his tail, not caring a bit what anyone said!

Julian looked at his compass as he went, and walked due south for some time. Then Aily gave a call, and pointed to the right.

'That way, that way,' she said.

'She wants us to go westwards now,' said Julian, stopping. 'I wonder if she's right. By my reckoning we're going dead straight for Old Towers now – but we shall be going up the hill to the right of it, if we go *her* way.'

'That way, that way,' repeated Aily, imperiously, and Dai barked as if to say she was right!

'Better follow her way,' said Dick. 'She seems so jolly certain of it.'

So Julian swerved to the right a little, and the others followed. They went a good way up the steep hill, and Julian began to pant.

'Is it far now?' he asked Aily, who was petting her lamb, and apparently taking no notice of the way they were going. Not that there was anything much to take notice of except snow on the ground and snowflakes in the air!

Aily looked up. Then she pointed again, a little more to the right, and said something in Welsh, nodding her head.

'Well – it looks as if we're getting near this place of hers – this "big, big hole", whatever it is,' said Julian, and on he went.

In about a minute Aily suddenly leapt off the toboggan and stood there, looking round with a frown.

'Here,' she said. 'Big hole here.'

'Well – it may be – but I'd like to see it a bit more *clearly*, Aily,' said Julian. Aily began to scrape down through the snow, and Timmy and Dai obligingly went to help her, imagining that she was after rabbits or a hidden hare.

'I'm afraid the poor kid's led us on a wild-goose chase,' said Dick. 'Why *should* there be a big hole here?'

Timmy and Aily had now got down through the snow to the buried clumps of heather that grew all over the slopes of the mountains in that district. Julian could see the clumps sticking up, stiff and wiry, in the clearing that Aily and the dogs had made.

'Timmy – you take Timmy!' said Aily, suddenly to George. 'He'll fall down, down – he'll fall like Dai one day – down, down!'

'I *say*! I believe she's looking for an old pot-hole!' said Dick, suddenly. 'You know – those strange holes that are sometimes found on moors – sudden holes that drop right down underground. They're called dean-holes I think, in some places. We found one once on Kirrin Island – don't you remember?'

'Oh *yes* – that was in the heather too!' said George, remembering. 'And it led to a cave below, by the seashore! *That's* what Aily meant by a big, big hole! A pot-hole on the moors! Timmy – for goodness sake come away – you may drop right down it!'

Timmy very nearly *did* go down the hole! George just caught his collar in time! But Dai was wary – he had fallen down once before!

'Hole!' said Aily, pleased. 'Big, big hole! Aily find for you!'

'Well – certainly you've found your hole – but how does it get us into Old Towers?' said Dick. Aily didn't understand. She knelt there, looking down at the hole she had uncovered under the heather and the snow.

'I must say that was a marvellous feat,' said Julian. 'Coming straight to this place and finding the hole when she couldn't see a thing through the falling snow. She really is as good as a dog. Good little Aily bach!'

Aily gave one of her sudden smiles, and slipped her hand in Julian's.

'Go down, yes?' she said. 'Aily show way?'

'Well – we'd better go down if it's possible,' said Julian, not much liking the idea, for he could see nothing but darkness inside the hole, and had no idea of what lay below.

Fany the lamb was tired of waiting about. She gave a little leap to the edge of the big round hole, and then put her small head in. She kicked up her heels – and was gone!

'She's jumped into the hole!' said George, amazed. 'Here, wait, Aily – you can't jump too – you'll hurt yourself!'

But Aily slithered into the hole, then let herself go.

'Aily here,' came a small voice from below. 'You come quick!'

18   Inside Old Towers

'Well! Did you see that – she just let go and dropped!'
said George, amazed. 'I wonder she didn't break her
legs. Julian, shine your torch down.'

Julian shone it down.

'It's a pretty good drop,' he said. 'I think we'll take
the ropes off our toboggans and let ourselves down on
those. I don't particularly want to break a leg or sprain
an ankle just at present.'

'If we pull our toboggans over the hole, and let their
ropes hang down into it, they will hold us safely,' said
Dick, and pulled his toboggan right across the hole.

Then Julian pulled the other toboggan across as
well, and soon the ropes were dangling down, ready
to take each of the four children.

'What about Timmy?' asked George, anxiously.
'Dai has jumped down – though I wonder *he* didn't
break a leg!'

'I'll wrap my coat over him and tie one of the ropes
round him,' said Julian. 'Then we can let him down
easily. Come here, Tim.'

Tim was soon tied up in the coat with the rope.
Then Dick slithered down on another rope, and stood
on the floor of the hole, ready to take Timmy when
Julian let him down. It really wasn't very difficult.
Aily looked rather scornful as the four children used
the ropes.

Julian laughed, and patted her shoulder.

'We're not all goat-like, you know,' he said. 'We don't gambol about the mountains all day long, like you, Aily. Well – that was your big, big hole. What next?'

He shone his torch round.

'Yes – it's a pot-hole. There's a small underground cave here. Look – is that a tunnel leading out of it?'

'Yes,' said George, as Aily and the lamb skipped off together down into the darkness of the tunnel. 'Look at that – no torch, no lamp – and yet she goes off into the darkness without any fear! I'd be scared stiff!'

'She's got eyes like a cat,' said Anne. 'Well, do we follow her? We'd better or we shall lose her!'

'Come on, Timmy,' said George, and all Five went down the dark, winding little tunnel after Aily. Anne glanced up at the rocky roof and thought with wonder of the thick masses of heather growing on its upper surface, all covered with thick snow.

Aily was nowhere to be seen! Julian grew worried.

'Aily! Come back!'

But there was no answer.

'Never mind,' said Dick. 'There's probably only one way to go, and she knows we must take it! If we come to a fork, we'll shout again.'

But they didn't come to a fork. The tunnel wound on and on, going steadily downhill. Its roof was of rock, and so were the walls, but underfoot was sandy soil alternating with rock ridges that made the going rather rough.

Julian looked at his compass.

'We've been going in a north-easterly direction more or less,' he said. 'And that *should* be in the direction of Old Towers. I think *I* know how Aily gets into the house!'

'Yes – this tunnel must pass right under the fence-that-bites, and under the grounds, and end somewhere near the cellars of the house,' said Dick. 'Or possibly *in* them. Where *is* that child?'

They caught sight of her just then, in the light of Julian's torch. She was waiting for them in a corner of the passage with Dai and Fany.

She pointed upwards.

'Way to garden!' she said. 'Little hole there – big for Aily! Not for you!'

Julian shone his torch upwards. Sure enough there was a small hole there, which appeared to be over-grown with weeds or heather – he couldn't tell what. He looked at the rocky sides of the upward passage to the hole, and saw how easily Aily could have climbed up to squeeze out of it, and roam the gardens! So that was how it was she had been able to pick up the notes that the poor old woman had thrown out so hopefully! Aily must surely have been the only person who managed to get into the grounds without permission!

'This way,' said Aily, and led them past the garden-hole and downwards again.

'We must be under the house now,' said Julian. 'I wonder if . . .'

But before he could finish his sentence he saw that the passage had led them into some old, half-ruined cellars. It went through a half-fallen cellar wall, and Aily proudly led them into a dark, cluttered-up cellar which, with its many barrels and old bottles, must once have been the wine-cellar.

'What cellars!' exclaimed Dick, in amazement, as they went through one after another. 'Dozens of them. Hey – what's this, Aily?'

He had come to where one high wall had been broken down completely – but the breakage seemed to have been done by human hands, for the breaks looked new, and were not covered with grime and mould as were the other fallen-down walls. A vast opening had been made into what seemed at first glance to be a low-walled cave.

Then a curious sound came to their ears. The sound of water – water gurgling and splashing! Julian took a step forward to peer into the cave beyond the broken walls.

But Aily tugged at his hand in terror.

'No, no! Not go there! Bad men, very bad men. Bad place there!'

'I say, look!' said Julian, amazed, taking no notice of Aily's tugging hand. 'An underground river –not just a stream – a *river*! Flowing down through the mountain, probably fed by springs on the way – and I bet it goes right down to the sea somewhere! We know the sea isn't far away!'

'Bad men down there,' said Aily, in panic, pulling back Dick and George too. 'Bang-bang – big fires – big noise. Come into the house, quick!'

'Gosh – isn't this extraordinary!' said Julian, quite astounded. 'What *is* going on here? We really shall have to find out. What in the world does Aily mean?'

Anne and George were astonished too, but had no desire to go along the river and find out!

'Better leave this for now, and go up into the house,' said George. 'After all, the old lady is the important thing at the moment. No wonder they imprisoned her in one of the towers, so that she wouldn't know what is going on!'

'Well, I'm blowed if *I* know what's going on,' said Dick. 'I'm not quite sure if I'm in some peculiar kind of nightmare or not!'

'Come into the house,' said Aily again, and this time, to her great relief, they followed her, Timmy trotting at the back with George, not quite knowing what to make of it all.

Aily led them unerringly back through the smashed walls, through the musty cellars, and into some that looked as if they had recently been used for store-places. Tins of food stood about, old furniture, old tins and baths and cans, barrels of all sizes and shapes.

'We go soft!' said Aily, meaning that they were now to walk quietly. They followed her up a long flight of stone cellar steps to a great door that stood half open. Aily stood at the top listening – probably for the tall caretaker, Julian thought. He wondered if the fierce dog was anywhere about the house. He whispered to Aily.

'Big dog in house, Aily?'

'No, big dog in garden, big dog there all day and night,' whispered back the little girl, and Julian felt most relieved.

'Aily find man,' said Aily, and shot off by herself, motioning to the others to wait.

'She's gone to find out where the caretaker is,' said Julian. 'My word – did you ever know anyone like her? Gosh, she's back again already!'

So she was, smiling mischievously all over her face.

'Man asleep,' she said. 'Man safe.' She took them through the door from the cellar into a perfectly enormous kitchen, with a colossal range at one end, black and empty now. A larger door nearby was open and Aily darted into it. She brought out a meat pie and offered it to Julian. He shook his head at once.

'No. You mustn't steal!' he said. But Aily either didn't understand, or didn't want to, for she bit into the pie herself, gobbling great pieces down, and then put it on the floor for the animals to finish, which they were very pleased to do!

'Aily – take us to the old woman,' said Dick, not wanting to waste time on things like this. 'Aily – you are *sure* there is no one else in the house?'

'Aily know!' said the little girl. 'One man to watch – he in there!' and she pointed towards the door of a nearby room. 'He watch old woman, and dog watch garden. Other men don't come in here.'

'Oh – well, where do *they* live then, these strange "other men"?' asked Julian, but Aily didn't understand. She led them to a great hall, from which two wide stairways swept up, meeting above at an even wider landing.

The lamb gambolled up, and the little dog Dai barked joyfully.

'Sh!' said all the four children at once, but Aily laughed. She seemed quite at home in the house and Dick wondered how many times she had let herself down into the pot-hole and come wandering in here. No wonder she spent so many nights away from home – she could always come and hide away in some corner of this big house! They followed her up the wide stairs.

But Aily would come no farther than the second floor. She had brought them up two flights of stairs – and now before them stretched a great picture gallery, that led to another stairway at the far end. The child hung back and refused to take Julian's hand.

'What's the matter?' he asked.

'Aily not come here before,' said the child, shrinking back. 'Not come here, not ever. Those people see Aily!' And she pointed at the rows of great pictures, each a portrait of some long-dead owner of the house.

'She's afraid of the portraits!' said Anne. 'Afraid of all their eyes following her as she runs down the long gallery! Funny little thing. All right – you stay here,

Aily. We'll go on up to the towers.'

They left Aily curled up behind a curtain, with Dai and Fany. Anne glanced at the rows of grave portraits as the four of them, with Timmy, walked softly down the long gallery. She shivered a little, for their eyes seemed to follow her as she passed, looking grave and disapproving.

Up another flight of stairs, and yet another. And now they were in a long passage that ran from tower-room to tower-room. Which was the tower they wanted?

It was very easy to find out! All of them had their doors wide open but one!

'This must be it!' said Julian, and knocked at the door.

'Who knocks?' said a weak, sorrowful voice. 'Surely not you, Matthew – you have no manners! Unlock the door and do not mock me with your knocking!'

'The key's in the door,' said Dick. 'Unlock it, Julian – quick!'

19   A lot of excitement

Julian turned the key in the lock and opened the door. A stately old woman sat in a chair beside the window, reading a book. She did not turn round.

'And why have you come at this time of the morning, Matthew?' she said, without turning round. 'And how did you find the manners to knock? Are you remembering the time when you knew how to behave to your elders and betters?'

'It isn't Matthew,' said Julian. 'It's us – we've come to set you free.'

The old woman turned at once, gaping in amazement. She got up and went over to the door, and the Five saw that she was trembling.

'Who are you? Let me out of that door before Matthew comes! Let me out, I tell you!'

She pushed by the four children and the dog, and then stood uncertainly in the passage.

'What shall I do? Where shall I go? Are those men here still?'

She went back into her room and sank down in her chair again, covering her face with her hands.

'I feel faint. Get me some water.'

Anne sprang to pour out a glass of water from a jug on a table. The old woman took it and drank it. She looked at Anne.

'Who are you? What is the meaning of this? Where is Matthew? Oh, I must be going mad!'

'Mrs Thomas – you *are* Mrs Thomas, aren't you?' said Julian. 'Little Aily, the shepherd's daughter, brought us here. She knew you were locked up. You remember her mother, don't you? She told us she used to work for you.'

'Aily's mother – Maggy – yes, yes. But what has Aily to do with this? I don't believe it. It's another trick. Where are the men who killed my son?'

Julian looked at Dick. It was clear that the poor old lady was not herself – or else this sudden appearance of the children had upset her.

'Those men that my Llewellyn brought here – they wanted to buy my house,' she said. 'But I wouldn't sell it, no, I wouldn't. Do you know what they said to me? They said that in this hill, far, far below my house, was a rare metal – a powerful metal – worth a fortune. What did they call it now?'

She looked at the children, as if expecting them to know. She shook her head as they didn't answer.

'Why should you know about it – you are only children. But I wouldn't sell it – no, I wouldn't sell my house – nor the metal below. Do you know what they wanted it for? For bombs to kill people with! And I said NO, never will I sell this place so that men can dig the metal and make bombs. It is against the law of God, I said, and I, Bronwen Thomas, will not do such a thing!'

The children listened in awe. The old lady seemed beside herself, and rocked to and fro as she spoke.

'So they asked my son, and he said no, as I had. But they took him away and killed him – and now they are at work below. Yes, yes, I hear them – I hear the noises creeping up, I feel my house shake, I see strange things. But who are you? And where is Matthew? He keeps me here, locked in my room. He told me about

Llewellyn, my poor dead son; he is a wicked man, Matthew, he works with those men, those evil men!'

She seemed to forget the four children for a little while. They wondered what to do. Julian saw that the poor woman was not fit to take down the stairs with them, and through the tunnel – and certainly she could not get out of the pot-hole. He began to wish that he hadn't been so hasty in his ideas of rescue. It would really be best to lock the door again and leave her here in safety until he could get the police – for certainly now the police must come.

'We will leave you now,' he said, 'and send someone soon to bring you out of here. We are sorry we disturbed you.'

And, to the astonishment of the others, he pushed them out of the room, turned the key in the lock again, and put it into his pocket!

'Aren't we going to take her with us?' said George, surprised. 'Poor, poor old thing!'

'No. How can we?' said Julian, troubled. 'We must go to the police, no matter what Morgan says. I see it all now, don't you? The mother forbidding the son to sell the old place, in spite of the enormous amount of money offered – the son refusing too – and the men making a plot to get in somehow and down to this metal, whatever it is – and work it . . .'

'And killing the son?' said Dick. 'Well, it may be so – but I should have thought that was a pretty drastic thing to do! Surely the son would have been reported missing very quickly, and the police would have made inquiries. Nobody said the son was missing or dead, did they, except the old lady?'

'Well, let's not talk about it now,' said Julian. 'We've got to *do* something. I'm sorry to leave old Mrs Thomas still locked up in that room, but I honestly think she would be safer there than anywhere else.'

They went down the two flights of stairs to the picture gallery. Aily was there, still cuddling her two pets. She was pleased to see them, and ran up smiling. She didn't seem to notice that they hadn't the old woman with them.

'Man down there very cross!' she said, and laughed. 'He awake now – he shout and bang!'

'Goodness – I hope he won't see us,' said Julian. 'We've got to get out of here, quick, and go to the police. Let's hope he won't come rushing at us, or call in that fierce dog.'

They went downstairs at top speed, looking out for Matthew. But there was no sign of him in person – though there was a most tremendous row going on somewhere, of shouting and banging.

'Aily lock door,' said Aily, suddenly, pointing in the direction of the sounds. 'Man lock old woman – Aily lock man!'

'*Did* you? Did you *really* lock him in?' said Julian, delighted. 'You really are a monkey – but what a good idea! I wish *I'd* thought of it!'

He went to the door of the room in which the angry Matthew was.

'Matthew!' he called sternly. There was a dead silence, and then Matthew's astonished voice came through the shut door.

'Who's that? Who locked me in? If it's one of you men, you'll be sorry for it! Silly joke to play on me, when you know I've got to go up and see to Old Mrs Thomas!'

'Matthew – this isn't one of the men,' said Julian, and how the others admired his cool, determined voice! 'We have come to rescue Mrs Thomas from that tower – and now we are going to the police to report

all this, and to report too that her son has been killed by
the men who are working far below this house.

There was an astonished silence. Then Matthew's
voice came again.

'What's all this? I don't understand! The *police* can't
do anything. Llewellyn, the son, isn't dead – my
word, no, he's all alive and kicking – and won't be
very pleased with *you*, whoever you are. Clear off at
once – but let me out before you go. I'm surprised that
Alsatian outside didn't get you, that I am!'

It was the children's turn to be amazed now. So the
son *wasn't* dead! Then where was he? And why had
Matthew told old Mrs Thomas such a cruel untruth?
Julian asked him at once.

'Why did you tell Mrs Thomas her son was dead
then?'

'What's it to do with you? Llewellyn told me to tell
his mother that. The old lady wouldn't let him sell that
stuff deep down under the house – the stuff that gets
hold of cars and bicycles, and ploughs, and makes
them heavy as lead. Magnetises them, so they say.
Well, if *he* wants to sell it, why shouldn't he? But what
I say is this – he shouldn't sell it to foreigners, no, that
he shouldn't! If I'd have known that – well – I wouldn't
have taken money from him to act like I did!'

The voice rose and fell as Matthew told his extraordinary tale. Then the man banged frantically on the
door again.

'Who are you? You let me out! I've been kind to the
old lady – you ask her – though she's difficult, and
strange in her ways. I've been loyal to Llewellyn,
though he's not easy, no, that he's not. Who are you, I
say? Let me out, let me out! If Llewellyn catches me
locked in here, he'll kill me! He'll say I've let his secret
out. He'll say . . . LET ME OUT, I say!'

'He sounds a bit mad,' said Julian, thankful that the man was locked up. 'He must be a bit simple too, to believe all that the son told him, and do everything he was told to do. Well – we'd better go to the police. Come on – we'll go back the way we came.'

'Let's just have a look down that river to see what the men are up to,' said Dick. 'Just you and I, Julian. It's such a chance – we needn't be seen, and it would only take a few minutes. The girls could wait somewhere with Tim.'

'I don't think we ought to stop now,' said Julian, 'I really don't.'

'No, don't let's,' said Anne. 'I don't like this house. It's got a horrid feel about it. And I can't *imagine* what the "shuddering" would be like, when the men start their work again, deep down below – whatever it is!'

'Well, come along then,' said Julian, and, completely ignoring Matthew's yells and bangs, the children made their way through the kitchen and down the cellar steps, flashing on their torches to light their way.

'I bet Matthew is wild that we've left him locked up,' said Dick, as they went through the vast cellars. 'Serves him right! Taking bribes from the son – and telling lies to that poor old woman. Hallo, we've come to where the men smashed the walls here to get along the river tunnel. I suppose they found that was the easiest way to go down to where the precious metal was – whatever it is!'

They stood looking through the smashed walls at the gurgling river.

'Come come,' said Aily, dragging at Julian's hand. 'Bad men there!'

She was holding Dai, her little dog, in case he fell into the rushing river, but Fany the lamb was gambolling loose as usual. And, quite suddenly, she skipped off down the river tunnel, her tail whisking behind her madly.

'Fany, Fany!' cried Aily. 'Fany come back!'

But the lamb, thinking that she was going the right way, gambolled on, deafened by the rushing of the water. Aily ran after her, as sure-footed as the lamb, hopping and skipping over the rough, rocky bank of the river.

'Come back!' yelled Julian. But Aily either did not or would not hear, and she disappeared into the blackness of the tunnel almost at once.

'She hasn't got a torch, Ju – she'll fall in and drown!' yelled George in a panic. 'Timmy, go after her. Fetch her back!'

And away went Timmy obediently, running as fast as he could beside the black, churning water, hurrying on its way downwards to the sea.

Julian and the others waited anxiously. Aily didn't come back, nor did any of the animals – and George began to be very panicky about Timmy.

'Oh, Julian – what's happened to Tim – and Aily?' she said. 'With no torch – oh, why did I let Timmy go? We all ought to have gone!'

'They'll come back all right,' said Julian, much more confidently than he felt. 'That child Aily can see in the dark, I really do believe – and she knows her way about like a dog.'

But when, after five minutes, not one of the four had come back, George started forward, flashing her torch on the rocky path beside the river.

'I'm going to find Timmy,' she said. 'And nobody's going to stop me!'

And she was gone before the boys could get hold of her! Julian gave a shout of aggravation.

'George! Don't be stupid! Timmy will find his own way back. Don't go down there – you don't know what you may find!'

'Come on,' said Dick, starting off down the river too. 'George won't come back, we know that – not unless she finds Tim and the others. We'd better go quickly before anything awful happens!'

Anne had to follow the boys, her heart beating fast. What a thing to happen! Just the very worst possible!

20   *In the heart of the hill*

It seemed like a bad dream to the four children, making their way over the rocky edge of the underground river. Their torches had good batteries, fortunately, and gave a bright light, so that they could see their way alongside the river. But at times this rocky 'path' they had to walk on grew very narrow indeed!

'Oh dear!' thought Anne, trying to keep up with the boys, 'I know I shall slip! I wish I hadn't these heavy snow-boots on. What a noise the river makes, booming along, and how fast it goes!'

Some way in front of the two boys and Anne was George, still calling for Timmy. She was very worried because he didn't come back to her, as he always did when she called him. She didn't realise that Timmy couldn't hear her! The river made such a noise in the enclosed rocky tunnel that Timmy heard nothing at all but the sound of the churning waters!

Quite suddenly the tunnel widened tremendously – the river making a big, broad pool before it tore on down the tunnel again. The walls opened out into an enormous cave, half of which was water and the other half a stretch of rough, rocky floor. George was most astonished. But she was even more astonished at other things she saw!

Two rafts, sturdy and immensely strong, were moored at the side of the deep pool! And on the floor of the cave were what looked like tin barrels, standing in rough rows – presumably waiting to be packed on to the rafts.

At one side of the cave were stacked great heaps of tins and bottles and cans, none of them opened – and on the other side an equally vast heap of discarded ones – all opened and thrown to one side. Big wooden crates stood about too – though George could not imagine what they were for.

The cave was dimly lit by electricity of some kind – probably from a battery fixed up somewhere. Nobody seemed to be about at all! George gave a call, hoping that Timmy was somewhere there.

'Timmy! Where are you?'

'And at once Timmy came from behind one of the big crates, his tail wagging hard! George was so glad that she fell on one knee and hugged him tight.

'You naughty dog,' she said, fondling him. 'Why didn't you come when you were called? Did you find the others? Where is Aily?'

A small face peeped from behind the crate nearby, the one from which Timmy had appeared. It was Aily. She looked terrified, and tears were on her cheeks. She clasped her lamb to her, and Dai was at her heels. She ran straight across to George, crying out something in Welsh, pointing back up the tunnel. George nodded.

'Yes. We'll go back straightaway! Look – here come the others!'

Aily had already seen them. She ran to Julian with a cry of delight, and he swung her up in his arms, lamb and all. He was very glad to see George and Timmy too.

They all had a good look round the strange cave.

I see what the idea is,' said Julian. 'Jolly clever too! They are mining that precious metal down here somewhere – and putting it on those rafts there, so that the underground river can take it right down to the sea. I bet they've got barges or something waiting down at some secret creek, to take the stuff away at night!'

'Whew!' said Dick. 'Very ingenious! And they count on the strange noises and shudderings and things to frighten people and keep them away from this hill – nobody dares to come prying round to see what's up!'

'The nearest farm is Magga Glen Farm, where the Joneses live,' said Julian. 'They would really be the only people who could find out anything definite.'

'Which they obviously did!' said Dick. 'I bet Morgan knows all about this, and is in with the son who sold the precious metal to the men who came after it – though it was his mother's.'

'There's no strange noise or anything down here – no noise at all except the sound of the river,' said Julian. 'Do you suppose the works aren't going just now?'

'Well,' began Dick, and then suddenly stopped as Dai and Timmy began to growl, Timmy in a deep voice and Dai in a smaller one. Julian at once pulled Aily and George behind a big crate, and Dick pushed Anne there. They listened intently. What had the dogs heard? Was there time to rush back to the tunnel and make their way out before they were seen?

Timmy went on growling in a low voice. The children's hearts began to beat fast – and then they heard voices. Where did they come from? Dick peeped cautiously round the crate. It was in a dark corner and he hoped he could not be seen.

The voices seemed to come from the direction of the great pool, and Dick looked over to it. He gave a sudden exclamation.

'Ju! Look over there! Do you see what *I* see?'

Julian looked – and was filled with astonishment. Two men had come *up* the tunnel, from the sea – evidently walking on the rocky edge of the river, just as they themselves had done – and were now wading in the shallows of the pool.

'One is *MORGAN*!' whispered Julian. 'And who's the other man! Gosh! – it's the shepherd – Aily's father! Would you believe it? Well – we always thought *Morgan* was mixed up in this – but I didn't think the shepherd was.'

Aily had seen both Morgan and her father. She made no move to go to the shepherd – she was far too scared of Morgan!

Morgan and the shepherd stood and gazed round a little, as if looking for someone. Then, keeping to the shadows, they made their way across the great cave right to the back of it, where another tunnel, very wide, led downwards into the hill.

As they went, a strange noise began.

'The rumbling!' whispered George, and Timmy growled again. 'But oh – doesn't it sound near. What a terrific noise – it's got right inside my head!'

It was no use whispering now! They had to shout if they wanted to say anything. and then the shuddering began! Everything shuddered and vibrated, and when the children touched one another, they could feel the vibration in the other's hands and arms.

'It's as if we're being run by electricity ourselves!' said Dick, astonished. 'I wonder if it's anything to do with that strange metal that is under this hill – that makes steel things heavy, so that ploughs won't plough, and spades won't dig!'

'Let's follow Morgan and the shepherd,' said Julian, so excited now that he felt he must see everything possible. 'We can keep well in the shadows. Nobody would ever guess we were here!'

'Aily – you stay here,' said Julian. 'Big noise, big, big noise frighten Fany and Dai.'

Aily nodded. She settled down behind the crate with her pets.

'Aily wait,' she said. She had no desire at all to go any nearer that strange noise! In her mind she imagined that possibly the thunder itself came from this hill and was made here. Yes, perhaps the lightning too!

Morgan and the shepherd had now disappeared into the tunnel right at the back of the cave, on the opposite side to the great pool. The Five went quickly over to it and looked down. It was very wide and very steep – but rough steps had been cut in it, so that it was not difficult to go down.

They trod warily down the steep tunnel, astonished because it was dimly lit – and yet there were no lamps of any sort to be seen.

'I think it's the reflection of some great glare far below,' shouted Julian, above the rumbling. The noise was so loud that it was almost like walking in the middle of thunder.

Down and down they went, and the tunnel curved and wound about, always steep, rocky and dimly lit. Suddenly the noise grew louder, and the tunnel grew lighter. The children saw the end of it, the exit outlined in brilliant light – a light that shimmered and shook in a most curious way.

'We're coming to the works – the mine – where that strange metal is!' shouted Dick, so excited that he felt his hands trembling. 'Be careful we aren't seen. JU! BE CAREFUL WE AREN'T SEEN!'

They went cautiously to the end of the tunnel and peered out. They were looking into a vast pit of light, round which men stood, working some curious-looking machines. The children could not make out what they were – and, indeed, the light was so blinding that it was only possible to look with their eyelids almost closed. All the men were wearing face-guards.

Suddenly the loud rumbling stopped and the light disappeared as if someone had turned off an electric switch! Then, in the darkness, a glow formed, a strange glow that came upwards and outwards, and seemed to go right through the roof itself! Dick clutched at Julian.

'That's the kind of glow we saw the other night!' he said. 'My word – it begins down here, goes right up through the hill in some strange way, and hangs above it! That shimmering must come from here too – some kind of rays that can go through anything – like X-rays or something!'

'It's like a dream,' said Anne, feeling George to make sure it wasn't! 'Just like a dream!'

'Where are Morgan and the shepherd?' said Dick. 'Look – there they are – in that corner, not far off. Look out – they're coming back!'

The four children moved back quickly into the tunnel, afraid of being seen. They suddenly heard shouts, and stumbled up the rocky steps even faster. *Had* they been seen? It sounded like it!

'I can hear someone coming up the tunnel behind us!' panted Dick. 'Quick, quick! I wish that noise would begin again. I know we can be heard!'

Someone was climbing swiftly up behind them. There were shouts and yells from below too. It sounded as if all the men were disturbed and angry. Why, oh why had they followed Morgan and the shepherd? They could so easily have gone back to the cellars!

They came to the top of the steep rocky tunnel at last, and ran to hide behind the crates, hoping to slip into the river-tunnel without being seen. They had to get Aily before they fled! Where was she?

'Aily, Aily!' shouted Julian. 'Where's she gone? We daren't leave her here. AILY!'

It was difficult to remember exactly where they had left her, in this great cave.

'There's the lamb!' cried Julian, thankfully, as he saw it on the other side of a crate. 'AILY!'

'Look out! There's Morgan!' shouted George, as the big farmer came out of the tunnel and ran across the cave. He saw the children and stopped in the utmost amazement.

'What are you doing here?' he roared. 'Come with us, quickly! You're in danger!'

The shepherd now appeared too, and Aily ran from behind her crate to him. He stared as if he could not believe his eyes, and then picked her up, calling something to Morgan in Welsh.

Morgan swung round on Julian again.

'I told you not to interfere!' he roared. 'I was handling this! Now we shall all be caught! Fool of a boy! Quick – we must hide and hope that the men will think we've gone down the tunnel. If we try to escape now, they will overtake us, and bring us back!'

He swept the astonished children into a dark corner and pulled crates round them.

'Stay there!' he said. 'We will do what we can!'

21 An astounding thing

The five children crouched behind the pile of crates. Morgan pushed another crate up, so that they were completely hidden. Dick clutched Julian.

'Julian! We've made fools of ourselves! Morgan was trying to find out the secret of Old Towers himself – with the help of the shepherd! They were about the only people in the neighbourhood who could guess what was going on. The shepherd could see all the strange things *we* saw, while watching his sheep on the mountainside – and he told Morgan . . .'

Julian groaned.

'Yes. No wonder he was angry when he thought we were meddling in such a serious matter. No wonder he forbade us to do anything more! Gosh – we've been idiots! Where is Morgan now? Can you see him?'

'No. He's hiding somewhere. Listen – here come the men!' said Dick. 'There's a crack between two crates here – I can see the first man. He's got an iron bar or something. He looks pretty grim!'

The men came out cautiously, evidently not sure how many people they were after. They advanced across the cave, seven of them, all with weapons of some kind. Two went to the upper river tunnel, two went to the one that led down to the sea, and the others began to hunt among the crates.

They found the children first! It was Aily's fault, poor child. She gave a sudden scream of fright – and in a trice the man had pulled away the crates. Crash – one by one they fell to the ground – and the amazed men found themselves looking at five children! But not for long! With a terrifying bark Timmy flung himself on the first man!

He yelled and began to fight him off, but Timmy held on like grim death. Morgan appeared from the shadows and surprised another of the men, jumping on him and getting him on the ground, at the same time catching hold of a second man and tossing him away. He had the strength of a giant!

'Run!' he yelled to the children, but they couldn't. Two of the men had penned them into a corner, and although Julian leapt at one of them, he was simply thrown back again. These men were strong miners, and though not a match for the giantlike Morgan, they could certainly take everyone else prisoner – including the gentle shepherd! He too was penned into a corner – only Morgan and Timmy were fighting now.

'Timmy will be hurt,' said George, in a trembling voice, and she tried to push one of the men away to get to him. 'Oh look, Ju – that man is trying to hit him with that bar!'

Timmy dodged the bar and sprang at the man, who turned and ran for his life. Timmy shot after him and got him on the ground. But there were too many men – and more were now coming up from the tunnel at the back of the cave, pouring in, with weapons of all kinds. All of them were amazed to see the five children!

The men seemed mostly to be foreigners, and spoke a language the children couldn't understand. But one man was not a foreigner – he was obviously the boss, and gave his orders as if he expected them to be obeyed. He hadn't joined in the fight at all.

The shepherd was soon overpowered, and his hands bound behind his back. Morgan fought for some time – but then had to surrender. He was like an angry bull, stamping here, pulling there, roaring with rage as three men tried to tie his hands.

The boss came up and faced him.

'You will be sorry for this, Morgan,' he said. 'All our lives we have been enemies – you down at the farm – and I here at Old Towers.'

Morgan suddenly spat at him.

'Where is your old mother?' he shouted. 'A prisoner in her own house! Who has robbed her? You, Llewellyn Thomas!' Then he went off into a spate of Welsh, his voice rising high as he denounced the man in front of him.

Julian admired the fearless Morgan enormously, as he stood with his hands bound, defying the man who had been a life-long enemy. How many quarrels had these two had, living in the same countryside, trying their strength against one another? Julian wished intensely that he had obeyed Morgan's command and left everything to him. But he had thought Morgan was on the side of the enemy! How stupid he had been!

'It's all because of us that he's caught,' thought the boy, remorsefully. 'I've been a fool – and I thought I was doing something clever – and right! And now we're all landed in this mess – the girls too! What will they do with us? I suppose the only *safe* thing for them to do is to keep us prisoner till they've finished this mining job, collected a fortune from the metal, whatever it is, and gone.'

Llewellyn Thomas was now giving some sharp orders, and the men were listening. Timmy was growling, held by the collar in a stranglehold by one of the men. If he tried to squirm away, the man twisted his hand in the collar a little more and poor Timmy was half-choked.

George was wild with despair. Julian had to keep stopping her from trying to make a dash to Timmy. He was afraid that these rough men would strike her. Aily sat in a corner, hugging her lamb and Dai, who had been far too scared even to take a *little* nip at any of the men!

Morgan was held by two hefty miners – but, quite suddenly, he hurled himself sidways at one of them and sent him flying – and then at the other, who staggered away and fell over a tin.

With a great roar Morgan stumbled to the pool, and waded to the entrance of the tunnel that led to the sea, his hands still tightly tied behind his back.

'The fool!' said Llewellyn Thomas. 'If he thinks he can get along that tunnel with his hands tied, he is mad! He will fall into that rushing river – and without his hands to help him, he will drown! No – don't go after him. Let him go – let him drown! We shall be well rid of him!'

The shepherd struggled to his feet to go after his master, knowing quite well that Llewellyn was right – no man could get along that rough edge to the river without his hands to steady him, feeling along the wall at the side – and one slip would put him into the churning, hurrying river, that ran at full-pelt down to the sea far below, at the bottom of the hill.

But Morgan did not mean to escape. He was not going to struggle along beside that treacherous torrent! He had come all the way up beside it, with the shepherd, and knew how easy it was to slip on the wet rocky edge. No – Morgan had another plan!

Julian watched him disappear into the tunnel, and his heart sank. He too knew that no one could walk along there without free hands to help him. But what could anyone do?

The boss turned to the other men, who were still staring after Morgan. He was just about to say something to them, when a roar came to their ears.

Not the roar of the torrent in the underground tunnel. Nor the roar of the strange rumbling mine. No – the roar of a giant voice, that crashed out of the tunnel, and echoed round the cave.

It was Morgan's enormous voice. Morgan, calling the names of his seven great dogs! The children listened in amazement to this unbelievable voice.

'DAI! BOB! TANG! COME TO ME! DOON! JOLL! RAFE! HAL!'

The names echoed round and round the cave, and it seemed as if the place was full of giant voices. Aily, who was used to hearing the dogs called, didn't turn a hair – but the others crouched back in amazement at the sound of such a voice. Surely no one in all the world had ever shouted so loudly before!

'DAI! DAI! RAFE! RAFE!'

The great voice boomed again and again, seeming to be louder each time. At first Llewellyn Thomas, the boss, was taken aback – but then he laughed sneeringly.

'Does he think he can get his dogs up from the beach?' he said. 'All that way down the tunnel. He's mad! Let him be!'

Then again the great voice roared out the names of the seven dogs belonging to Morgan and the shepherd.

DAI! BOB! TANG! DOON! JOLL! RAFE! HAL!'

At the last name, Morgan's voice seemed to crack. The shepherd raised his head in dismay. Morgan had overstrained that great voice of his, and no wonder. No megaphone could possibly have been louder!

There was silence after that, Morgan called no more. Neither did he appear again. The children felt scared and depressed, and Aily began to whimper.

The curious shuddering vibration began to creep into everything again, and the boss turned sharply, giving some more orders. Two of the men ran to the tunnel at the back of the cave and disappeared. Then things took on a curious shimmer, as if a heat-haze had spread everywhere, and it began to feel very warm in the cave.

Suddenly something happened. At first it sounded far off in the distance, a confused noise that made Timmy tug at his collar again and prick his ears. He barked, and the man who was holding him hit him.

'What's that noise?' said Llewellyn Thomas, sharply, looking all round. There was no telling where it came from. But it grew louder – and louder – and then suddenly Julian knew what it was!

It was the loud barking of seven angry dogs! The shepherd knew it too, and a glad smile came over his face. He glanced at Llewellyn to see if he recognised it as well.

Yes – the boss had certainly recognised that dreadful sound now. He could hardly believe it! Surely it was not possible that Morgan's voice, enormous as it was, had echoed all the way down the tunnel, and been heard by the sharp, pricked-up ears of the dogs who loved him?

But so it was! Dai, the oldest dog, who loved his master more than any of them, had stood tense and listening ever since Morgan and the shepherd had left them. And, from somewhere far distant, echoing down to the end of the tunnel they were guarding, Dai had heard the faint echoes of his master's beloved voice!

His bark had told the other dogs the news – and, led by Dai, they had all rushed up the rocky tunnel, sure-footed on the slippery, rocky path beside the racing river.

They came to Morgan, sitting beside the river, not far from the big cave, a little way down the tunnel. It was a moment of joy for Morgan and his dogs!

Dai soon snuffed at his hands and bit the ropes in half. Morgan was free!

'Down now – and hush!' commanded Morgan. He began to walk steadily back to the cave, then motioned the dogs before him.

'Attack!' he cried in Welsh.

And then, to the men's horror, the seven dogs raced out of the tunnel at a great speed, barking, growling, snarling – with a triumphant Morgan behind them, so tall that he had to bend double to leave the tunnel.

The men fled, every one of them. Llewellyn had turned to run even before the dogs appeared, and was gone. Dai leapt at one man and got him down, and Tang leapt at another. The cave was filled with snarls and growls and excited barking.

Timmy delightedly joined in, for his captor had rushed away too. Even little Dai ran to join this wonderful fight, while the children stood amazed and thankful to see their enemy defeated!

'Who would have thought of this?' said Dick, sending the crates crashing down. 'What an *astounding* thing! Hurrah for Morgan and his seven dogs!'

22 · All's well that ends well!

Morgan would not let the children stay underground any longer.

'We have things to do,' he said, in his deep voice, which sounded rather hoarse now. 'You will go back to the farm and telephone to the police for me. You will say "Morgan has won" and tell them to send a boat to the little creek I have already told them of. There I will bring these men all the way down the tunnel to the sea. Go now, at once. Obey me this time, boy.'

'Yes,' said Julian. This man was a hero! And he had thought him a villain! He was ready to obey his smallest command now. Then a thought struck him, and he turned back.

'The old woman,' he said. 'Mrs Thomas – that man's mother. What about her? And we've locked the caretaker up in his room!'

'You will not do anything but go to the farm and telephone,' said Morgan, sternly. 'I will do everything there is to be done. Take Aily with you to the farm. She must not be here. Now *go*.'

And Julian went! He and the others took one last look round at the men, all pinioned by the dogs, lying still and panic-stricken. Then, with Aily and her lamb and dog, he led the others up the tunnel again, and at last back into the cellars.

'I don't like leaving that old lady up there, in the tower,' said Dick.

'No. But obviously Morgan has his plans,' said Julian, who was not going to disobey orders in any way this time. 'I expect he has arranged something with the police. We can't interfere now. We messed things up a bit, I'm afraid.'

They climbed soberly up to the place where they had left their toboggans. It took them some time, and they were beginning to feel very hungry. But Julian wouldn't let them stop even to eat some sandwiches.

'No,' he said. 'I've to telephone to the police as soon as ever I can. No stopping now! We'll munch our sandwiches on the way down to the farm.'

It wasn't very difficult to get out of the pot-hole, for they had left the ropes dangling down. Julian and Dick helped the two girls up by pushing them, and they in turn helped to pull up the boys from the top of the hole.

Aily scrambled up easily, swinging delightedly on a rope, and then flinging herself out of the hole. The lamb leapt up in a miraculous manner, and Julian handed Dai to the small girl.

Timmy was hauled up in the same way as he had been let down. He had badly wanted to stay with the other dogs – but nothing would make him leave George!

'Well, that's that,' said Julian, scrambling out last of all. 'Now let's see. We could toboggan down this slope, and halfway up our own slope. That would save a lot of time. Aily, you're to come with us to the farm.'

'No,' said Aily.

'Yes, Aily bach,' said Julian. 'I want you to.' He took her small hand in his and she smiled her sudden little smile, quite content to go along with this big kind boy, even though she was afraid of going down to the farm for fear she should meet her mother.

'Aily good girl,' said Julian, setting the little thing on his toboggan.

They tobogganed down the slope at a great speed without any mishap, and halfway up the opposite slope. It seemed odd to be out in the dazzling daylight after the dark tunnels underground. Their adventure below began to seem slightly unreal!

'We'll leave the toboggans at the hut,' said Julian, as they dragged them up the rest of the slope. 'Anyone thirsty? I am. I think it must be something to do with that mine – my mouth got as dry as anything as soon as we were down there.'

Everyone said the same.

'I'll run into the hut and pour out some orangeade,' said Anne. 'You stack the toboggans in their place, Ju, and just see if there's enough oil in the can out in the bunker – we'll need to fill the stove tonight. And if there isn't enough we must bring some up with us.'

Julian gave her the key of the hut and she unlocked it and went in with George. They poured orangeade into five cups, and drank thirstily. Their mouths were drier than they had ever been before! Anne felt thankful that she didn't have to wait any longer for a drink.

'I think the roof of my mouth would have stuck to my tongue!' she said, putting down her cup. 'That was lovely!'

'There's plenty of oil,' reported Julian, coming to drink his orangeade. 'My word – I needed this. I'd not like to work down in that mine.'

They locked the hut and set off down to the farm, munching their sandwiches hungrily. They tasted very good indeed, and even Aily asked for one after another. Timmy had his share, and once they missed him, and had to stop and call him.

'Has he lost his bit of meat in the snow?' wondered Anne. But no – he, like the rest of them, was suffering from a very dry mouth and was busy licking the snow, letting it melt in his mouth and trickle down his dry throat!

Mrs Jones was most surprised to see them. When she heard Julian's request to telephone to the police, she looked worried.

'It's all right, Mrs Jones,' said Julian, comfortingly. 'It's a message to them from Morgan. Everything is fine. We'll tell you what's happened as soon as he comes home. He might not like us to say anything till then!'

The police did not seem at all surprised to hear Julian's message – they appeared to be expecting it!

'We will see to the matter,' said the sergeant, in his deep, stolid voice. 'Thank you.' And he rang off at once. Julian wondered what would happen next – what had Morgan arranged?

They were pleased to see Mrs Jones bringing in bowls of hot chicken soup, as they sat talking round the wood fire she had hurriedly lit in the living room.

'Oh! Just what we feel like!' said Anne, gratefully. 'I'm still awfully thirsty – aren't you, George? And look, Timmy – there's a nice meaty bone for you! You *are* kind, Mrs Jones!'

'You know – I feel pretty awful about all this now,' said Julian. 'We shouldn't have interfered after Morgan said we weren't to. I wish we hadn't. He can't think much of us!'

'I vote we all apologise humbly,' said Dick. 'How *could* we have thought he was the villain of the piece? I know he's dour and silent – but he didn't look mean or cruel.'

'We'd better stay down here at the farm till Morgan comes back,' said George. 'Quite apart from wanting to say I'm sorry, I'd like to know what happened!'

'So would I,' said Anne. 'And Aily ought to wait for her father. He'll want to know that she's safe.'

So they asked Mrs Jones if they could stay till Morgan came home. She was delighted.

'Of course, now,' she said. 'We've a roasting turkey today – and you shall come and have supper with us in our room for a change!'

This all sounded rather good. The children gathered round their fire to talk, and Timmy rested his head on George's knee. She looked at his neck.

'That man almost choked him,' she said. 'Oh look, Julian – he's bruised all round his poor neck!'

'Now don't start moaning over Timmy's neck again, for goodness sake!' said Dick. 'Honestly, George, I'm sure Tim thinks the adventure was worth a bruised neck! *He's* not grumbling. He was jolly brave, I think – and didn't he enjoy himself when the other dogs rushed into the cave, and he joined in the fight!'

'I wonder what they'll do about that poor old woman,' said Anne. 'She will be glad her son is alive, I suppose – but what a shock for her to know he'd lied to her, and sold what is really hers – that strange metal under the hill!'

'Well – I imagine it won't be allowed to be sold now,' said Julian. 'What a plan that was! To get men up that tunnel to mine the stuff – and to send it down by rafts to waiting ships, hidden in that creek. We ought to go down and examine the creek – it would be interesting to see what sort of a place it is down there.

It must be well hidden in a fold of the cliff, I should think.'

'Yes – let's do that tomorrow,' said George, thrilled. 'I vote we stay here tonight. I feel tired after such an adventure! Don't you?'

'I do a bit,' said Julian. 'Well – I suppose there won't be quite so much shuddering and shimmering and rumbling now! Funny that that hill should always have been so peculiar, isn't it – "ploughs that will not plough, spades that will not dig!" Must be some kind of iron, I suppose, that magnetises things. Oh well – it's all beyond me!'

Morgan came back with the shepherd when it was dark. Julian went straight up to the burly farmer.

'We want to apologise for being such idiots,' he said. 'We shouldn't have interfered after what you said.'

Morgan gave a broad smile. He seemed to be in a very good humour indeed.

'Forget it, boy,' he said. 'All's well now. The police came up the river tunnel, and all the men are safe in jail. Llewellyn Thomas is a sad man tonight. His mother is free and is staying with friends – poor lady, she doesn't understand what has happened, and that is as well. And maybe now the right people will get that strange metal – it's worth a hundred times its weight in gold!'

'Come in for your supper, Morgan bach, and shepherd too!' said Mrs Jones, in her lilting voice. 'The children are coming too. We've a roasting turkey – it's your birthday, Morgan boy!'

'Well there now, I didn't know it!' said Morgan and gave his mother such a hug that she squealed. 'Let's go in to the turkey. I've had nothing all day.'

Soon they were all sitting down before the most enormous turkey that the children had ever seen in their lives! Morgan carved it swiftly. Then he said something to his mother in Welsh and she smiled and nodded.

'Yes, you do that,' she said.

Morgan collected some slices of turkey on a big enamel dish, and then went to the door that led from the living room into the farmyard. He roared loudly and the children jumped. What a voice!

'DAI! TANG! BOB! DOON! RAFE! JOLL! HAL!'

'He's calling the dogs,' said Anne. 'Just as he called them up the tunnel. Well – they certainly deserve a good dinner!'

Then down to the door came the seven dogs, jostling each other, barking excitedly. Morgan threw them the slices of turkey, and they gobbled the tasty bits up greedily.

'Woof!' said Timmy politely from behind him, and Morgan turned. He solemnly cut a big slice and a little slice.

'Here!' he said to Timmy and little Dai. 'You did well too! Catch!'

'There'll not be much left of your birthday turkey!' said his mother, half-cross, half-amused. 'Now fill your glasses again, children, and we will drink to my Morgan – a better son there never was!'

Anne poured home-made lemonade into the empty glasses, while Morgan sat and smiled, listening to his seven dogs still barking together outside.

'Happy birthday, happy birthday!' shouted everyone, raising their glasses, and Julian added his own few words.

'Happy birthday – and may your voice NEVER grow less!'

Number Crunchers
Brain
Bafflers

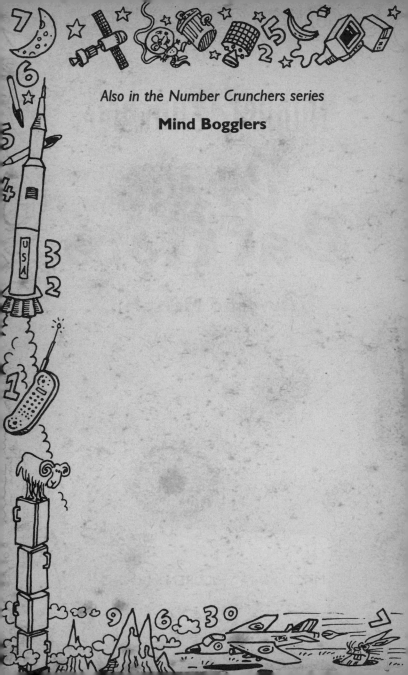

Also in the Number Crunchers series

Mind Bogglers

Number Crunchers

Brain Bafflers

Rowland Morgan

MACMILLAN CHILDREN'S BOOKS

First published 1998
by Macmillan Children's Books
a division of Macmillan Publishers Ltd
25 Eccleston Place, London SW1W 9NF
and Basingstoke

Associated companies throughout the world

ISBN 0 330 36783 8

1 3 5 7 9 8 6 4 2

A CIP catalogue record for this book is available from
the British Library.

Printed by Mackays of Chatham plc, Chatham, Kent.

Introduction

Have you noticed that numbers are everywhere? Every motor vehicle has one (buses have several). So does every telephone, every house, every address, every publication. Nearly all products now carry a bar-code, which represents a number. Everything has its price, which is another number. And everything digital, from compact discs to computers, works by numbers (1 and 0).

People have numbers, too. In fact, they have a long string of them. Take my case: I have a birth certificate number, a driver's licence number, a passport number, a national insurance number, a tax number, a national savings number, a current bank account number, a joint account number with my wife, plus Switch cards for each account, a telephone number, plus telephone customer number, a gas account number, an electricity account number, a fax number and an Internet number, plus a telephone charge account number, a video library card number, a library card number, and a snooker club membership number. That's just the basics.

There are plenty more.

So, attached to my identity there is a basic string of numbers. Yes, I am a string of about 150 digits. Like everyone else, though, I look after number one.

Statistics

Those identifying numbers are codes. If you had the right key, you could work out a lot of interesting stuff. For example, the telephone company can match its customer account numbers with phone numbers and find out all sorts of things about where people are and how they behave.

That's where computers come in. The main reason numbers are multiplying is computers. They can handle numbers phenomenally fast. For example, they flash billions of units of money round the world's electronic stock markets in microseconds. They can also store and interpret numbers in a way that was never dreamt of before.

The Office of National Statistics can survey all Britain's households in a few seconds, using information gathered in the census and stored in a database. The Office found that less than a quarter (24 per cent) of households are now traditional families made up of a married couple living with their children.

Another organization (the Rowntree Foundation), used computers to work out that the cost of raising a child to the age of 17 is about £50,000. Because another computer survey showed that parents typically raise 1.9 children, it means they spend

$$1.9 \times 50,000 = 95,000$$

no less than £95,000 on their kids!

Calculators

Notice that calculation above?

To do it, I used a British invention, a miniature electronic calculator (first marketed by Sir Clive Sinclair). The calculator is a machine that does sums. But, depending on who is using it, it can make numbers come to life. For example, that survey of the cost of raising a child could have given the annual figure

$$50,000 \div 17 = 2,941$$

But £2,941 is not an impressive enough amount of money. A round £50,000 packs more punch.

That's the enjoyment of number-crunching. You can get high impact. For example, everyone goes to bed at night. It's a routine we hardly think about. But check how much you sleep in a year, counting nine hours a night.

$9 \times 365 = 3{,}285$

Now convert that 3,285 hours into 24-hour days, then months, counting 30 days per month:

$3{,}285 \div 24 = 136.8 \ (139) \text{ days}$

$139 \div 30 = 4.6 \text{ months}$

Four months a year: it is strange to think that we lie sprawled on a bed, dead to the world, for that long. It's even stranger that in a typical lifetime of about 70 years, we lie flat out, slumbering and snoring for

$70 \times 4 = 280 \div 12 = 23.3 \ (23) \text{ years}$

no fewer than twenty-three years. We're all Sleeping Beauties.

Number Crunching

Number crunching means getting enjoyment out of a calculator. It's the art of using statistics to express facts in an interesting way.

For example, *Jaws* is a frightening film that comes near the top of the all-time box office hits, but if you look up the figures and divide them into each other, for every human killed by a shark, about 4.5 million sharks are killed by humans. That puts a fresh spin on it.

Here's another: you can use your calculator and some trade statistics to show that Americans throw away about 4.4 million so-called 'disposable' ballpoint pens a day. It's a big number, but hard to picture. Why not measure a ballpoint? You'll find it's about 15 centimetres long with the top on (weight 15 grammes). Then work out how far those non-biodegradable thrown-away ballpoints would stretch, laid end-to-end. Fifteen centimetres is 0.15 of a metre. It goes like this:

4,400,000 x 0.15 = 660,000 (metres) ÷ 1,000 = 660

So, the pen dump would stretch 660

kilometres, or 413 miles, which is further than Nottingham to Aberdeen, and would take

$$413 \div 70 = 5.9$$

nearly six hours to drive along at top speed.

This book contains 78 number crunchings that I've done for you. The statistics I used are provided in a **Statpak**. If the fact is laid out as a multiple selection, you can guess the right answer, and then work out whether you got it right. Other facts you can choose to believe or not, and then work out whether they're true.

A note on huge numbers

Like the world's human population, numbers are getting bigger all the time. Your calculator will probably handle eight figures, that means a maximum of 99,999,999. If you are calculating billions (1,000,000,000, also known as a thousand million) you may need to drop one set of noughts, as in the following operation:

$$7,001,000 \, (000) \div 365 = 19,180 \, (000)$$
$$= 19,180,000 \div 2,300,000 = 8.339$$

In order to fit the billions in, you drop three

noughts, and add them on as soon as they will fit onto the LCD screen. In the above operation, you add them on in the second calculation.

Rounding: Numbers rounded up, or down, are shown in brackets, or after an equals sign like this: 48.9 = 50.

Sample Big Numbers

World foreign exchange dealings are estimated at £812 billion *per day*.

The Ministry of Agriculture has 182 animal health inspectors for 10.2 million cattle and 43 million sheep – or 292,000 per inspector.

UK cars and vans could jam up Britain's 3,100 km of motorways more than 22 times over.

The Niagara Falls could fill an Olympic swimming pool more than twice a second.

British factories produce more than 13 cars a minute.

Units

To express today's huge statistics in a way that is easier to picture than strings of figures, we use big visual units. Here's a list of the main ones with their facts and figures.

Unit List

SUPERTANKER
Load: 100,000 tonnes
The world fleet of supertankers is approximately 800. Three thousand smaller tankers have a combined cargo capacity of 263 million tonnes. The total tanker fleet capacity is about 360m tonnes.

JUGGERNAUT LORRY
Average load: 23 tonnes
16 metres long
There are 79,000 38-tonne articulated lorries in Britain. They could jam up a six-lane motorway for 210 kilometres, or 130 miles, further than London to Birmingham. They can carry between 20 and 24 tonnes of freight.

ROAD TANKER
30,000 litres/
6,600 gallons

JUMBO JET
370 passengers
Cruising speed: 917 kph/570 mph
Cruising altitude: 10,668 metres/35,000 feet

AIRSHIP
105,000 cubic metres of gas/
3,700,000 cubic feet

HOT AIR BALLOON
2,180 cubic metres/77,000 cubic feet
The air in a Montgolfier hot air
balloon of the "77" championship
type weighs between three and
four tonnes.

BUSLOAD
50 people

TITANIC
52,250 tonnes
2,435 people

EIFFEL TOWER
300 metres high
8,757 tonnes

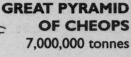

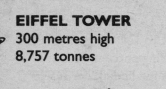

GREAT PYRAMID
OF CHEOPS
7,000,000 tonnes

POWER STATION
2,000 megawatts/2 gigawatts

OLYMPIC SWIMMING POOL
2,300 cubic metres (2,300,000 litres/
506,000 gallons)

ROUND THE WORLD
40,075 kilometres/24,902 miles

EARTH TO THE MOON
382,000 kilometres/
237,000 miles
(average)

Percentage increase per year

Companies always want to sell you more, so they are forever measuring percentage increases. A useful trick for finding out how many years it will take for an amount to double is to divide its annual percentage increase into 70. So, a five per cent annual increase means that the annual amount will double in $70 \div 5 = 14$ years.

A note on your calculator

The mind-blowers in this book are for crunching numbers, not brains. They are meant to blow minds, not fuses. A standard calculator will do. You need not worry about a GCSE calculator or A-level calculator. If you are using an advanced calculator, you will have to remember the BODMAS formula which governs the order in which calculations are made.

True or false?

Your neighbour is 98.2 per cent brainless.

Statpak

Brain's average percentage of human bodyweight: 1.8

Guinness Book of Records

Take your pick

In a fuel shortage, vehicles could form a queue

1) 6 metres
2) 600 metres
3) 6.5 kilometres long

at every British petrol station.

Statpak

Petrol stations: 18,500
Vehicles on UK roads: 30,000,000
Average vehicle length: 4 metres

Shell UK Ltd/DVLA

Take your pick

People in Britain drink more than

1) two
2) two hundred
3) eight

Olympic swimming pools of pop per day.

Statpak

Pop consumption per year:
7,001,000,000 litres

Water in an Olympic swimming
pool: 2,300,000 litres (506,000
gallons)

Trade statistics

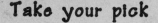

Take your pick

When rockets launch a satellite into orbit, they rip a hole in the protective ozone layer. On average, they have gashed the ozone layer once every

1) 4
2) 44
3) 444

days since 1957.

Statpak

Known successful satellite launches
1957 – 1998: 3,670
Days in a year: 365

Royal Aircraft Establishment

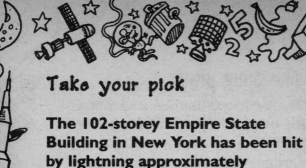

Take your pick

The 102-storey Empire State Building in New York has been hit by lightning approximately

1) 13
2) 134
3) 1,340

times since it was built in 1931.

Statpak

Average number of times per year that the Empire State Building is hit by lightning: 20

Krantz, L., America By The Numbers

Take your pick

National Health Service surgeons perform

1) more than seven
2) more than 70
3) nearly 0.7

operations a minute.

Statpak

Operations carried out per year: 4 million

Days in a year: 365

Hansard vol 240/80 (2) Col 1051

Take your pick

On an average day, Royal Air Force warplanes take

1) 3.44
2) 34.4
3) 344

low-flying trips over Britain.

Statpak

Minimum RAF low-flying sorties over Britain made since 1979: 2,390,000
Days in a year: 365

Hansard Vol 240/79 Col 732

Prove It!

Juggernaut lorries loaded with a year's chocolates and chocolate bars for Europeans would queue all the way across France.

Statpak

Europeans consume 2,000,000 tonnes of chocolates a year.
Calais (north French coast) to Marseilles (south French coast):
1,059 kilometres
Juggernaut load: 23 tonnes
Juggernaut length: 15 metres

Euromonitor

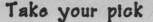

Take your pick

If the Chinese adopt British flying habits, the country will have

1) 0.33
2) 3.3
3) 33

polluting airliner flights per minute.

Statpak

Annual air transport movements for 58m Britons: 872,000
Times the People's Republic of China's population exceeds Britain's: 20

BAA plc

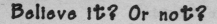

Believe It? Or not?

A seal travelled 167,000 times its own length across ice and snow before freezing.

Statpak

Number of kilometres from the shore of Antarctica that explorers found a frozen seal: 250
Seal length: 1.5m

Norwegian Polar Institute/New Scientist 1908

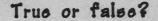

True or false?

It is 16 per cent cheaper to license an experimenter on animals than a car.

Statpak

Personal licence under the Animals (Scientific Procedures) Act 1986: £108
UK motor vehicle tax disc: £125

Hansard 235/26 col 336/Driver & Vehicle Licensing Centre

Prove it!

The police intend to computerize enough fingerprint records to cover more than a quarter of the male population.

Statpak

Non-retired male adults in Britain: 18,426,000
Fingerprint records intended to be held on the police computer: over 5,000,000

Whitaker's Almanack/HM Chief Inspector of Constabulary (NAFIS database by 2001; nearly all fingerprints will be male)

Believe It? Or not?

It would take pollution inspectors 85 years to visit all Britain's factory premises.

Statpak

Premises regulated by the Factory Inspectorate: 540,000
Inspections carried out by HM inspectors of pollution in one year: 6,327

Dept of the Environment health & safety executive/Dept of the Environment 1991-2 (Hansard 211,51)

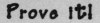

Prove it!

By the year 2001, there will be one robot for every 5,500 people in the world.

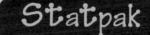

Statpak

Industrial robots expected to be installed worldwide by 2001:
1,000,000
World population: 5,500,000,000

United Nations

Take your pick

Every hour on Britain's motorways, drivers travel the equivalent of

1) 1.32
2) 13.2
3) 132

times round the world.

Statpak

Annual motorway mileage:
46,671,000,000

Lex Report on Motoring/MORI

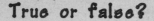

True or false?

On a given day, only one car in 15,000 gets stolen.

Average daily car thefts: 1,683
Private and light goods vehicles:
25,000,000

Home Office (Hansard 235/25 col 272)/Whitaker's Almanack

Prove it!

For every English subject Queen Elizabeth I had, Queen Elizabeth II has 12.

Statpak

Estimated English population in 1570, based on the number of baptisms, burials and marriages: 4,160,221
In 1997: 50,000,000

Whitaker's Almanack

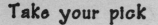

Take your pick

Non-biodegradable Barbie dolls sell at a rate of

1) 25
2) 2,500
3) 25,000

an hour.

Statpak

Sales of Barbie dolls per year:
63,072,000
Seven-day week
Seven-hour day

Mattel-Corgi

Believe It? Or not?

British people have 134 times more computers than Indians do.

Statpak

Computers per 1,000 population in
the United Kingdom: 134
In India: 1

Worldwatch Institute

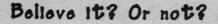

Believe it? Or not?

British people have half as many computers as Americans.

Statpak

Computers per 1,000 population in
the USA: 265
In the UK: 134

Worldwatch Institute

Believe It? Or not?

One in five British buses are defective.

Statpak

Passenger–carrying vehicles officially inspected in one year: 39,065
Found defective: 7,463

Dept of Transport, Hansard 236,36 col 388

Take your pick

At American rates of ownership, the world's households in 2010 would possess at least

1) 260,000
2) 2.6 million
3) 2.6 billion

kitchen cookers.

Statpak

Average number of people in a US household (94 million for 250 million population): 2.7

American households owning a cooker: 100 per cent

Predicted world population in 2010: 7,000,000,000

Author/Guinness Book of Answers 9th Edition/Predicast Forecasts

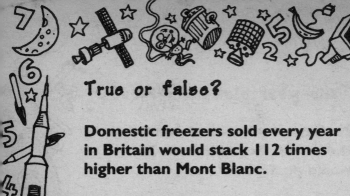

True or false?

Domestic freezers sold every year in Britain would stack 112 times higher than Mont Blanc.

Statpak

Annual UK home freezer sales:
600,000
Freezer height: 90cm
Metres altitude of Mont Blanc: 4,807

*Euromonitor Consumer Europe
1993/Whitaker's Almanack 1994*

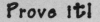

Prove It!

The British population is expected to increase by 12 busloads a day.

Statpak

UK population in 1998: 58,000,000
Population predicted in 2012: 61,000,000
Busload: 50

HMSO, Annual Abstract of Statistics/HMSO, Sustainable Development, the UK Strategy

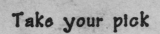

Take your pick

To design their new plane, Boeing engineers could have used a different computer terminal every

1) month
2) week
3) working day

for more than eight years.

Statpak

Computer workstations used simultaneously to design the forthcoming Boeing 777 airliner: 2,200

Workdays per year: 260

British Airways

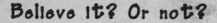

Believe it? Or not?

Of every five barrels of oil the world produces, two are used by Americans.

Statpak

Percentage of world oil consumption that is used by the USA: 40

Worldwatch Institute

True or false?

Population increase alone promises to add a 273-kilometre traffic queue of car users each year.

Statpak

Annual population increase predicted: 177,755
People per car now: 2.6
Length of car: 4 metres

HMSO Sustainable Development, the UK Strategy

38

Believe it? Or not?

One-quarter the population of Britain stands as good a chance of winning the national lottery jackpot as your family does.

Statpak

Lottery jackpot odds: 1 in 14 million
Population of Britain: 58 million

Camelot plc

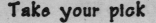

Take your pick

If you wanted to make a one-minute call to every telephone in Britain, it would take

a) 0.51
b) 51
c) 501

years.

Statpak

Telephones in Britain: 26,880,000

BT

40

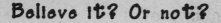

Believe It? Or not?

A year's banana crop weighs more than seven Egyptian pyramids.

Statpak

World annual banana crop:
49,630,000 tonnes
Great pyramid of Cheops: 7,000,000 tonnes

UN

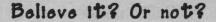

Believe It? Or not?

You could visit a different sweetshop in Britain every day for 141 years.

Statpak

Sweetshops (CTN) in Britain: 51,702

The Retail Rankings

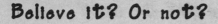

Believe it? Or not?

Crisps consumed each day weigh more than two jumbo jets.

Statpak

UK eats 30 million bags of crisps a day, weighing: 900 tonnes
Maximum take-off weight of jumbo jet: 372 tonnes

Walkers Crisps/BA

Believe it? Or not?

Over 37,000 corner shops could be fitted into Tesco supermarkets.

Statpak

Tesco sales area: 1,325,868 square metres (14,272,000 sq ft)
Corner shop sales area: 35 square metres (376 sq ft)

Tesco plc

Believe it? Or not?

The Flora margarine we eat each year weighs more than six Eiffel Towers.

Statpak

Weight of Flora margarine sold each year: 60,000 tonnes
Weight of the Eiffel Tower: 8,757 tonnes

Unilever

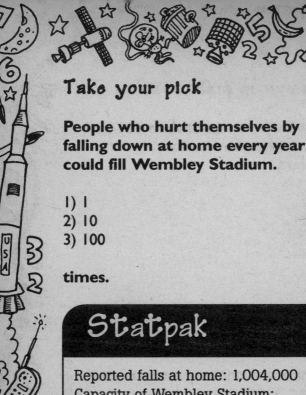

Take your pick

People who hurt themselves by falling down at home every year could fill Wembley Stadium.

1) 1
2) 10
3) 100

times.

Statpak

Reported falls at home: 1,004,000
Capacity of Wembley Stadium: 100,000

Home Office

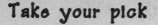

Take your pick

For every person alive in 1066, there are now:

1) 2.1
2) 21
3) 211

Statpak

Estimated world population in 1066: 254,000,000

In 1998: 5,500,000,000

UN

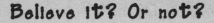

Believe it? Or not?

Sixty-nine Mars bars are consumed in Britain every daylight second.

Statpak

Mars bars eaten per day in Britain: 3,000,000

Cadbury-Schweppes

Believe it? Or not?

The world's population could fit into Devon.

Statpak

Square metres of Devon:
6,720,000,000
Estimated world population:
5,500,000,000

Hutchinson Guide to The World

Take your pick

If you saved a penny an hour for a year, you would have:

1) £1.87
2) £8.70
3) £87.60

Statpak

Days in the year: 365 (except leap years)

50

Take your pick

A perfect game in 10-pin bowling is

1) 100
2) 1000
3) 300

points.

Statpak

Points per pin: 1
Frames to a game: 10
Strike: 10 pins
Strikes possible per frame: 3

True or false?

The Beatles' performing fee multiplied by 65 times in a year.

Statpak

Fee paid by New York impresario to the Beatles for two shows in one day in 1964: $5,500
For one show in 1965: $180,000

John Glatt, Rage & Roll: Bill Graham and the Selling of Rock

True or false?

Every year, hunters in Italy killed more than twice as many songbirds as pet cats have ever killed altogether in Britain.

Statpak

Number of birds Britain's domestic cats are believed to have tormented and killed: 20,000,000
Songbirds killed by humans in Italy each year: 50,000,000

Hellenic Society for the Protection of Nature/National Audubon Society/World Watch magazine

Believe It? Or not?

If you weigh about 45 kilos (seven stone), you are nearly 30 litres of water.

Statpak

Percentage of human person which is water: 65

National Geographic

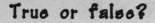

True or false?

A gas-fired electric power station wastes over half of its energy.

Statpak

Percentage energy efficiency of a gas-fired power station: 45

Dept of Employment Hansard 235,25 col 217

Believe It? Or not?

The fresh water consumption of fun-loving tourist destination Dade County, Florida, could empty 475 Olympic swimming pools every day.

Statpak

Average litres of water used by Dade County per day: 1,078,839,000
Volume of Olympic swimming pool: 2,270,000 litres

Miami Herald

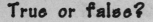

True or false?

A sight-seeing trip to visit one of the USA's dams every day would last over two centuries.

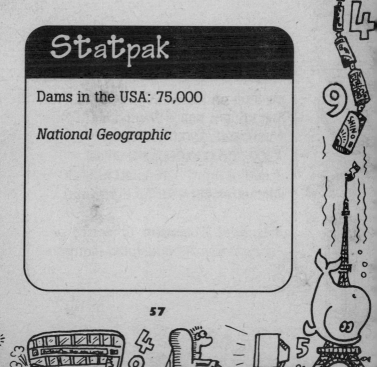

Statpak

Dams in the USA: 75,000

National Geographic

Believe It? Or not?

Even travelling at the speed of light, it would take more than 1,300 years to reach the first known planet outside our solar system.

Statpak

Distance in kilometres from Earth of first known Milky Way planet: 12,391,948,800,000,000 (or 7,700,000,000,000,000 miles)
Speed of light: 9,454,240,512,000 kilometres per year (or light year)

Alexander Wolzsczan, University of Pennsylvania/Philadelphia Inquirer

Take your pick

A potato has

1) more
2) fewer

chromosomes per cell than a human being.

Statpak

A potato's chromosomes per cell: 48
A human being's: 46

The Hutchinson Dictionary of Science, London 1994

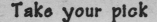

Take your pick

You are

1) 2
2) 15
3) 215

times more likely to be dealt an unbeatable hand at poker than to win the National Lottery jackpot.

Statpak

Odds on drawing a straight flush in 52-card draw poker: 1 in 64,974
On winning the National Lottery jackpot: 1 in 14,000,000

Camelot plc/Go Figure

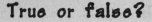

True or false?

Potatoes are 96 times more expensive when bought as a packet of crisps.

Statpak

Price of 0.45 kilograms of potatoes at the farm: 3.6p
Price of 0.45 kilograms of potatoes packaged as Golden Wonder crisps: £3.46

Food Miles, s.a.f.e. alliance (@ 26p per 34g packet)/New Covent Garden Market

Believe it? Or not?

For every penny it gave to charity, a top crisps company made more than £72 profit.

Statpak

Profits per £1.00 of published charity donation of the company: £7,274

A Guide to Company Giving 1993, The Directory of Social Change (UK)

True or false?

There are over four-and-a-half billion potential customers for quiet, non-polluting bicycles.

Statpak

Percentage of humanity who can afford to buy a car: 10

Percentage who can afford a bike: 80

World population: 5,700,000,000

Worldwatch Institute, Washington DC

Take your pick

The surface of planet Earth that is more than three kilometres under water could accommodate

1) 10
2) 100
3) over 1,000

United Kingdoms.

Statpak

Percentage of Earth's surface that is 3,000 metres or more below sea level: 50
Area of planet Earth's surface: 509,953,886 square kilometres
Area of Great Britain: 244,100 sq. km

Worldwatch Paper 116

True or false?

A sports team could play on a different Greater London playing field every Saturday for 100 years.

Statpak

Playing fields in Greater London: 5,191
Saturdays in a year: 52

Hansard Vol 239/71 col 908

Prove It!

Plastic packaging dumped by British households every year could load a quarter of all the juggernaut lorries in the country.

Statpak

Percentage of all used plastic consumer packaging that is recycled: 1–2

Tonnes of plastic packaging thrown away by households: 455,000

Tonnes carried by juggernaut lorry: 23

Juggernauts: see page 8

Materials Reclamation Weekly

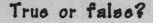

True or false?

Somebody escapes from prison every 40 hours.

Escapers from English and Welsh prisons in the 2,099 days between 20 June 1988 and 24 March 1994: 1,239

Hansard Vol 240/80 Col 941

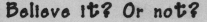

Believe it? Or not?

A year's rubbish from London could jam up all six lanes of a motorway with loaded juggernauts for over 1,700 kilometres.

Statpak

Tonnes of waste from London per year: 15,000,000
Tonnes carried by a juggernaut: 23
Length of a juggernaut: 16 metres
Motorway lanes: 6

RM/Warmer Bulletin 41

True or false?

When a child now 10 is a grown-up aged 35, more people will have been added to the world population than were alive on Earth before World War Two.

Statpak

US Census Bureau's estimate of world population: 5,700,000,000
Expected in 2020: 7,900,000,000
World population in 1933: 1,993,000,000

New Scientist 1924/Whitakers Almanack 1939

Believe it? Or not?

About 47 million people in Japan do without flush toilets.

Statpak

Percentage of Japanese residents
with flush toilets: 63
Japanese population: 128,000,000

OECD/Nature vol 369 no 6475

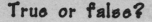

True or false?

New York City alone has nearly as many children in care as the whole of England.

Statpak

Children in foster care in New York: 51,000
Children looked after by local authorities in England: 55,000

The Economist vol 331 no 7863 (1990)/Health & Personal Social Services Statistics (England) 1993, DoH

True or false?

Aerosol cans emerging from UK factories each year could be littered nose-to-tail round the world five times.

Statpak

Aerosol cans made each year: 1,000,000,000 (including 58 million for hair mousse and 93 million for shaving soap)

Average length of an aerosol can: 20 centimetres

The world's circumference at the equator: 40,075 Kilometres/24,902 Miles

The Grocer

Believe it? Or not?

If the Chinese start eating as much chocolate as the British, each year they'll need more than 100 supertankers full.

Statpak

UK annual chocolate consumption: 500,000 tonnes
UK population: 58,000,000
Approximate Chinese population: 1,300,000,000
Supertanker load: see Units on page 8

Euromonitor/Hutchinson

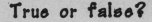

True or false?

The Indian sub-continent's tiger population is one-thirteenth what it was 60 years ago.

Statpak

Estimated sub-continental population of tigers in the 1930s: 40,000
Today: 3,000

Focus, The World In Perspective

74

Check it!

If young prisoners on remand paced the length of their cell half the time they were locked inside it, they would walk more than 100 kilometres a week.

Statpak

Daily hours in cell targeted for unconvicted prisoners: 18
Walking speed: 0.5 metre per second

Hansard vol 244 no 112 col 244 (Scotland)

Believe it? Or not?

Played continuously on one channel, British TV commercials booked to sell the video version of *Jurassic Park* would have lasted more than a month, round-the-clock.

Statpak

Hours of TV commercials booked for Jurassic Park: 800

Moving Pictures UK 189

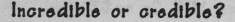

Incredible or credible?

In our national newspapers, sixty-eight times more is spent advertising cars than trains.

Statpak

Average daily motoring advertising expenditure in UK national newspapers: £491,000
Rail advertising: £7,202

Register-MEAL (£179.4m per year on cars, £2.6m on rail, not counting colour supplements)

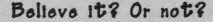

Believe it? Or not?

All the fresh Siberian leopard skins left in the universe would not buy a new Mercedes convertible.

Statpak

Estimated number of amur leopards left on the planet: 40
Sterling equivalent of price asked for amur leopardskin in a Vladivostock newspaper: £1,986
Cost of a Mercedes Benz SL600: £94,600
National Geographic Vol 185 no 6 (amur leopard)/Mercedes Benz (UK) Ltd

True or false?

Somebody calls the Child Support Agency every 77 seconds.

Statpak

Telephone calls per year on the Child Support Agency's national enquiry line: 676,018

Hansard vol 244 no 112 col 248

Believe It? Or not?

Unpolluted beluga whales can dive to a depth of nearly two Eiffel Towers, and still surface to breathe.

Statpak

Height of Eiffel Tower: 300 metres
Depth to which a Beluga whale can dive: 550 metres

*National Geographic Vol 185 No 6
(1,800 ft)*

Check for yourself

One page devoted to describing each species of life on earth would fill six kilometres (3.75 miles) of bookshelf.

Statpak

Mid-range estimate of number of species on Earth: 6,000,000
Thickness of piece of paper: 1 millimetre (0.001 of a metre)

New Scientist 1,925

Prove it!

A year of Europe's junked aerosol cans could easily stack to the Moon.

Statpak

Aerosol cans thrown away unrecycled every year: 2.55 billion
Average height of aerosol can: 16 centimetres (0.16 metre)
Moon's average distance: 382,000 kilometres (237,000 miles)

Aerosols: Recycling & Disposal, BAMA (aerosol 16 cm)/The Cambridge Concise Encyclopedia

Take your pick

A firm leaving its 200 desktop computers switched on all night would run up an electricity bill of

1) £22
2) £222
3) £22,000

a year.

Statpak

Cost of electricity used by a 120-watt desktop computer left on overnight: 30 pence

PC Magazine, February 1994 (Siemens-Nixdorf Green PC [50% on 50% idle, 5.8–99.4w])/Compaq advertising campaign for Deskpro XL4/66 model

True or false?

A two-piece silk suit requires about 20,000 silk worms to be boiled alive.

Statpak

Silk worms boiled alive to make a single silk garment: about 10,000

Tobias, M, Environmental Meditations (USA)

Take your pick

Pieces of space junk in orbit round Earth could double to 344,000 in

1) 10
2) 20
3) 40

years.

Statpak

Larger items of space junk in orbit: 172,000
Percentage annual rate of increase: 3.5 (see Doubling period calculation, Page 11)

NASA communique 27.vi.94 (based on 3.5 per cent annual growth)

Believe it? Or not?

A year's pay of one record company boss, if given in recorded music, would make a stack of compact discs higher than Mount Everest.

Statpak

Reported daily pay rate of the record company boss, including bonuses and awards: £50,000
Height of Mount Everest: 8,872 metres (29,118 ft)
Price of CD: £15
Thickness of cased CD: 1.1 centimetres (0.011 metre)
Working days in a year: 260
RM/The Guardian

Take your pick

A total of

1) two
2) three
3) eight

supertankers a week would be required to ship away the packaging wasted by Americans.

Statpak

Tonnes of packaging dumped by Americans in a year: 43,000,550 (47,400,000 US tons)
Supertanker load: 100,000 tonnes

The Coalition of Northeast Governors (1990)

True? Or false?

Someone born today who takes up watching three and a half hours of television a day from age five can expect to spend nearly 10 solid years in front of the TV screen before dying.

Statpak

Average life expectancy: 72
Daily hours of television viewing:
3.5

RM/BFI Film & TV Handbook

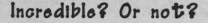

Incredible? Or not?

By the year 2005, British drivers can expect to be wasting 1,700 centuries a year sitting in stopped traffic.

Statpak

Hours expected to be spent in traffic jams by UK drivers in 2005: 1,500,000,000

Hawken, P, The Ecology of Commerce (pro rata)

Answers

12 $100 - 1.8 = 98.2$

13 $30,000,000 \div 18,500 = 1,621 \times 4 = 6,486 \div 1,000 =$
    $6.486 = 6.5$ km

14 $7,001,000\ (000) \div 365 = 19,180\ (000) \div 2,300\ (000) =$
    8.339

15 $1998 - 1957 = 41$ (years) $\times 365$ (days) $= 14,965 \div 3,670$
    (launches) $= 4$

16 $1998 - 1931 = 67 \times 20 = 1,340$

17 $4,000,000 \div 365 = 10,958 \div 24$ (hours) $= 456 \div 60$
    (minutes) $= 7.6$

18 $2,390,000 \div 19$ (years) $= 125,789 \div 365$ (days) $= 344$

19 $2,000,000 \div 23 = 86,956$ (lorries) $\times 15$ (length) $=$
    $1,304,347 \div 1,000 = 1,304$ kilometres

20 $872,000 \times 20 = 17,440,000 \div 365 = 47,780 \div 24 =$
    $1,990 \div 60 = 33$

21 $250 \times 1000 = 250,000 \div 1.5 = 166,666 = 167,000$

22 $125 - 108 = 17 \times 100 = 1700 \div 108 = 15.7 = 16$

23 $18,426,000 \div 5,000,000 = 3.68$ (i.e. over a quarter)

24 $540,000 \div 6,327 = 85$

25 $5,500$ (million) $\div 1$ (million) $= 5,500$

26 $46,671,000\ (000) \div 40,075 = 1,164\ (000) = 1,164,000 \div$
    $365 = 3,189$ (per day) $\div 24 = 132$ (per hour)

27 $25,000,000 \div 1,683 = 14,854 = 15,000$

28 $50,000,000 \div 4,160,221 = 12$

29 $63,072,000 \div 365 = 172,800$ (day) $\div 7 = 24,685$ (25,000)

30 $134 \div 1 = 134$

31 $265 \div 134 = 1.977$ (2)

32 $39,065 \div 7,463 = 5.23$

33 $7,000,000\ (000) \div 2.7 = 2,592,592$ (592) (2.6 billion)

34 $600,000 \times 0.9 = 540,000$ (metres) $\div 4,807 = 112.33$

35 $61,000,000 - 58,000,000 = 3,000,000 \div 14 = 214,285$
    (annual inc.) $\div 365 = 587$ (daily inc.) $\div 50$ (busload) $=$
    $11.78 = 12$

36 $2,200 \div 260$ (workdays) $= 8.46$ (years)

37 $100 \div 20$ (one-fifth of 100) $= 5$
    $40 \div 20$ (one-fifth of 100) $= 2$

38 $177,755 \div 2.6$ (people per car) $= 68,367 \times 4$ (car length)
    $= 273,469 \div 1000$ (kilometre) $= 273.4$

39	58,000,000 ÷ 14,000,000 = 4.1 (i.e. one-quarter)
40	26,880,000 ÷ 60 (minutes) = 448,000 (hours) ÷ 24 = 18,666 (days) ÷ 365 = 51
41	49,630,000 ÷ 7,000,000 = 7.09
42	51,702 ÷ 365 = 141.6
43	900 ÷ 372 = 2.4
44	1,325,868 ÷ 35 = 37,881
45	60,000 ÷ 8,757 = 6.85
46	1,004,000 ÷ 100,000 = 10.04
47	5,500 (million) ÷ 254 (million) = 21.6
48	3,000,000 ÷ 12 (daylight hours) = 250,000 ÷ 60 = 4166.6 ÷ 60 = 69
49	6,720 (000,000) ÷ 5,500 (000) = 1.2 (square metres each)
50	1 x 24 = 24 x 365 = 8,760 ÷ 100 = £87.6
51	10 + 10 + 10 = 30 x 10 = 300
52	5,500 ÷ 2 = 2,750 (per show) 180,000 ÷ 2,750 = 65.4
53	50,000,000 ÷ 20,000,000 = 2.5
54	45 x 65% = 29.25 (kilos/litres)
55	100 − 45 = 55 (per cent)
56	1,078,839 (000) ÷ 2,270 (000) = 475
57	75,000 ÷ 365 = 205.479 (years)
58	(approximation): 12,391 ÷ 9.45 = 1,311 (light years)
59	48 − 46 = 2
60	14,000,000 ÷ 64,974 = 215.47
61	346 ÷ 3.6 = 96.1
62	7,274 ÷ 100 = 72.74
63	5,700,000,000 x 80% = 4.560,000,000
64	509,953 (000) x 50% = 254,976 (000) ÷ 244 (000) = 1,044
65	5,191 ÷ 52 = 99.82 = 100
66	455,000 − 2% = 445,900 ÷ 23 = 19,386 79,000 ÷ 19,386 = 4 (i.e. a quarter)
67	2,099 x 24 (hours) = 50,376 ÷ 1,239 = 40.65
68	15,000,000 ÷ 23 = 652,173 x 16 = 10,434,768 ÷ 1000 = 10,434 ÷ 6 (lanes) = 1,739
69	7,900 (000,000) − 5,700 (000,000) = 2,200 (000,000) = 2,200,000,000
70	128,000 (000) x (100% − 63% = 37%) 37% = 47,360,000

71 55,000 − 51,000 = 4,000 × 100 = 400,000 ÷ 51,000 = 7.8 (percentage more in Britain)

72 1,000,000,0000 × 0.20 (metres) = 200,000,000 ÷ 1,000 = 200,000 ÷ 40,075 = 4.99 = 5

73 1,300 (000,000) ÷ 58 (000,000) = 22.4 × 500 (000) = 11,206 (000) ÷ 100 (000) = 112

74 40,000 ÷ 3,000 = 13.3

75 18 × 60 = 1,080 (minutes) × 60 = 64,800 (seconds) ÷ 2 = 32,400 (half the time) × 0.5 (metres) = 16,200 ÷ 1,000 = 16.2 (kilometres per day) × 7 = 113.4 kilometres per week

76 800 ÷ 24 (hours in a day) = 33.33 days

77 491,000 ÷ 7,202 = 68.17

78 1,986 × 40 = 79,440
    94,600 − 79,440 = 15,160

79 676,018 ÷ 365 (days in year) = 1,852 ÷ 24 (hours in day) = 77 ÷ 60 (minutes in hour) = 1.28 × 60 (seconds) = 76.8 (77)

80 550 ÷ 300 = 1.83

81 6,000,000 × 0.001 = 6,000 (metres) ÷ 1,000 = 6 (kilometres)

82 2,550,000 (000) × 0.16 = 408,000 (000) ÷ 1,000 = 408,000 (kilometres) ÷ 382,000 = 1.06

83 0.30 (£) × 200 = 60 × 365 = 21,900 (£22,000)

84 10,000 × 2 = 20,000

85 70 ÷ 3.5 = 20

86 50,000 × 260 (working days in a year) = 13,000,000 (£) ÷ 15 = 866,666 × 0.011 = 9,533 (metres)

87 43,000,550 ÷ 100,000 = 430 ÷ 52 = 8.27

88 72 − 4 (infancy) = 68 × 365 = 24,820 × 3.5 = 86,870 ÷ 24 = 3,619 (days' viewing) ÷ 365 = 9.9 = 10 (years' viewing)

89 1,500,000 (000) ÷ 24 = 62,500 (000) = 62,500,000 ÷ 365 = 171,232 (years) ÷ 100 = 1,712